Chapter One

Coventry's Annual Food Festival was already going much better than the Beltane Festival. The first day had been a roaring financial success for Craft Donuts, and the second promised to be even better. My employees were all working during the festivities, and I was on my way to pick up Auntie Lilith. She'd said she wanted to get to the festival early to make sure she got to sample the dishes she wanted most, and she thought it would be fun to go with me.

Probably because she knew I'd pay for everything, but my mother would have told her to come out of pocket if she wanted something. Mom and Lilith had a special bond, but that didn't mean my mother was a pushover for Lilith's… antics.

I pulled into her driveway and turned off the car. Meri stood up from the passenger seat and stretched lazily. He nearly dug his claws into the seat fabric, but I shot him a look that stopped him in his tracks. "I wasn't going to claw the seat."

"Sure," I said as I dropped my keys into my purse and snapped it closed.

I didn't know how he managed to fall asleep in the space of a few blocks, but sometimes he did. Probably because some nights, he stayed up all ni prowling for trouble. At least when he did that, he entertained himself.

As I got out of the car, Meri darted across the center console and then jumped to the driveway. He was already on the front porch waiting when I closed the driver's side door.

I adjusted my purse strap on my shoulder and walked gingerly across Lilith's flagstone path to her front steps. Not because they were booby-trapped, which they very well could be, but because I'd already caught a toe and tripped several times on previous visits. You'd think I'd have learned, but...

Sometimes I wondered if she'd deliberately made them as hazardous a possible. Like, was she out there in the moonlight moving them just a little bit to ensure that nobody could ever learn the least dangerous path across them?

That seemed paranoid, but it was Lilith we were talking about. Oh, and the stone pavers looked normal, but they were set just far enough apart that you couldn't traverse them without having to stretch a little extra. Especially if you were short... like most of her family.

I made it without faceplanting, and Lilith's front door swung open without a knock. Was she sitting behind the curtains in her front window waiting to see if I tripped and sprawled? I tried to remember if the curtains were closed when I got out of the car, or if they'd been open a crack. You know, just enough so she could watch me fall. I could see her there, curtains parted just enough for one eye to look out, waiting to laugh hysterically at my unfortunate tangle with gravity.

Surely not. Lilith embraced her dark side, and thoroughly enjoyed shadow work, but we all knew she'd never harm a member of her family. She would never revel in one of us banging a knee or smashing our noses.

Right…

"You're finally here!" Lilith gushed as she stepped back and allowed Meri and me to enter. "I was beginning to get worried."

"Lilith, I'm ten minutes early," I said and checked my watch again just to be sure.

Despite my early arrival, Lilith looked ready to go. She'd dressed in an ankle-length red velvet dress with a black vest layered over the top. Half of her long, silver hair was pulled into a bun on top of her head. The other half fell in soft waves around her shoulders, and she'd adorned her ears, wrists, and neck with silver moon jewelry.

"Anyway," she said and waved a hand, bracelets twinkling and clanking, through the air as if to dissipate my statement, "I'm all out of jimsonweed. I need you to run over to that store of yours and grab some for me. Unless you have some on you?"

"I don't have jimsonweed on me, Lilith. Why would I have something like that in my pocket? Or in my purse? Do you carry poison herbs on you? Wait, don't answer that."

She shrugged. "You never know. I don't judge. Do you have some at home then?"

"I don't keep poison plants in the house because of the girls. I know they're witches, but it's still not worth the risk," I answered.

Lilith waved her hand in the air again. "You shouldn't coddle them so much. They need to learn to handle their craft."

"They are in elementary school," I said. "And I certainly hope you aren't keeping that stuff within reach when they come visit you."

It wasn't entirely true. There might have been a poison plant or two around my house, but certainly not inside. Maybe in the garage… But it was not the kind of thing I just kept in my purse. I wasn't Lilith.

Lilith turned away and went back to what she was doing without a word. By that time, I'd followed her into the dining room. Her huge mahogany table was covered with an assortment of black crystals, candles, a sprinkling of black salt, and several aging parchments.

"Lilith? Have you been letting Hekate work with poison plants?" I asked even though I knew the answer already.

"A little belladonna tea never hurt anyone," she scoffed. "Those girls have got to learn how to properly handle all types of herbs and ingredients. I'm doing you a favor."

"Lilith!"

"Oh, this is good," Meri said as he sauntered into the room and plopped down between the two of us.

"Don't be such a Mary Sue," Lilith said as she dumped a vial of something black and smoky into a small brass cauldron. The tendrils wound out like it was attempting an escape, but she flicked some black salt at them.

"I'm not," I protested. "It's just that I'm not sure my very young daughters are quite ready for…"

"For what?" Lilith cut me off, and it was obvious I'd offended her.

"For this," I said and waved my hands around. "You don't exactly practice the safest forms of magic, and not everybody believes this stuff is necessary. I just want them to be old enough to handle it all."

"I don't know that Laney will ever be ready for it," Lilith admitted, "but that's why I don't work with her very much. Hekate, on the other hand, was born ready. And of any member of our coven, I am the one who is best prepared to decide when she's ready and train her in the shadow arts. This is my wheelhouse, Kinsley. And for Hekate, and other witches like her... like me, my practices are absolutely necessary. The balance must be maintained. What would happen to this world if we all just did safe, fluffy white magic? Sure, it might be great for a while, but we both know it would be the end."

I sighed. She was right, and I said as much. "You're right, Auntie. I'm sorry. I just worry about them."

"That's your job, Kinsley. You're their mom, so you worry. I'm the fun aunt, so I don't. Now, about that jimsonweed. How long will it take you to get some?"

"We're supposed to be going to the festival," I protested. "You wanted me to pick you up early, so I'm here early."

"And we will go, but I've got to finish this first. It's important."

"Okay," I relented. "I'll run to the shop and get you the jimsonweed, and then we can leave?"

"Of course," Lilith answered. "It's a good thing you showed up ten minutes early. We might not even be that far behind. I can always count on you."

I waited for a moment to see if there was anything else, or if she was going to pay for the ingredient, but Lilith was too busy adding extraordinarily tiny feathers to her mini cauldron. Her left hand was full of the feathers, each less than half an inch in length, and she'd pluck one with her right before dropping it into the cauldron. The smoky tentacles would grab the white plumes and drag them in like a predator devouring its prey.

She didn't even look up at me again. As I closed the front door behind me, she was muttering an incantation under her breath.

Meri and I traipsed down the front porch steps and across the path to the car, and that time, I managed to catch my toe and trip on the third flagstone paver. Fortunately, I righted myself without going all the way down. I dropped my purse, though. So, I bent over to pick it up, and then slung it back over my shoulder as I stood. I heard a neighbor's dog barking like crazy somewhere off in the distance, but when I looked around, no one was about.

I walked the rest of the way to my car and dug my keys out of my purse. As I hit the button to unlock the doors, the dog went silent.

"I'll drive!" Meri called out as I opened the driver's door.

For a moment, I thought he might be serious. He just laughed at my stricken expression and then hopped into the back seat.

"What am I, driving Miss Daisy?" I asked as I slid behind the wheel. "I didn't realize I was a chauffeur."

"You're driving me crazy," he retorted.

"Short trip."

I felt a big paw come around from behind and bop me on the forehead. Meri had climbed up the back of my seat and bonked me on the face.

"Hey, claws off my seats," I said and backed out of the driveway.

He must have gotten bored and decided to do whatever he'd climbed back there to do because I didn't get bopped again. I heard him moving around behind me as I drove, but I kept my eyes on the road.

"You might not be a chauffeur, but you're basically Lilith's errand girl," Meri said as I turned off Lilith's street onto one of the main roads.

"I am not. But you know how Lilith is. I might as well just get the jimsonweed so we can get on with our day. Once her mind is set on something, she won't pull herself away from it until she's done. It would have been nice if she'd texted me first. At least then, I could have saved myself the trip to her house and back out again."

As I pulled into a parking space in front of Summoned Goods & Sundries, Meri hopped into the front seat. I was about to ask him what the heck he was up to, but people were pouring into the town square. The festival had begun for the day, and I needed to get the jimsonweed and get back to Lilith. We had an entire day of gorging ourselves on the finest culinary delights Coventry had to offer, and I was excited.

When I walked into the shop, I was hit with a scent I didn't expect. The whole store smelled like freshly baked brownies. It was nearly overwhelming, but in a good way. Like a warm chocolatey hug.

It wasn't an unpleasant experience, but it was unexpected. Normally, Summoned Goods & Sundries had the vague smell of burning sage and hint of patchouli or basil. It never smelled like a bakery.

I had to remind myself that we were smack dab in the middle of a food festival. When I looked around for a moment, I discovered the source of the heavenly aroma.

Sol was up at the checkout counter digging into a gigantic brownie sundae. No, not just one. He had two of them. Huge bowls filled with chunks of freshly baked brownies topped with what looked like homemade French vanilla ice cream. A layer of hot fudge ran down the sides of the ice cream scoops like delicious lava, and on top of that was a generous sprinkle of colorful chocolate candies. All of it was topped off with whipped cream and a single maraschino cherry.

Sol grinned at me sheepishly. "This was not all for me. I bought one for Azura, but she only wanted a few bites."

"That's weird," I said. "She didn't like it? Because those look amazing. Are they not as good as they look?"

"She's been in a bad mood today."

I approached the counter and looked the brownie sundaes over. "Seems like those would help," I said, suddenly wishing I had one.

"That's what I thought. I figured that these would brighten her day, and maybe she wouldn't be in such a funk. I was wrong."

"Well, not to insult your lady love, or a very good employee, but when is Azura not in a bad mood? Being in a funk is kind of her default setting."

"No, it's not like that," Sol said. "Not like her usual gloom. I'm actually a little worried. She seemed… sad. Like genuinely sad. Not morose, but maybe a little devastated. But she won't tell me what's going on."

It almost made me smile that Sol knew Azura's various shades of blue so well. You could see that he genuinely cared for her. Maybe even loved her.

The problem was that if he was worried about her, then I was too. Azura was normally tough as nails. Up until that exact moment, I figured she could handle anything life threw at her. Sure, she might be moody about it, but she'd get through.

"Did she tell you what's wrong? I've never known Azura to hold back about something that's bothering her. She loves telling us what's bothering her."

"She said she didn't want to talk about it," Sol said and swallowed hard.

"Oh, wow. Okay," I said and started looking around for her.

"I had really hoped these brownie mountain supremes would cheer her up. Brownies always make things better. Even Azura likes chocolate, and it's hard to find things she likes."

"I'll talk to her," I said. "Where is she? She didn't leave, did she?"

"She's upstairs. Another customer was complaining about Estrella, so Azura took over."

"What this time?" I asked and then regretted it. "You know what? Never mind. Whatever it is, I don't want to know."

"If it means anything, I really do think the customer was being overly critical," Sol said cheerfully. "Maybe not Estrella's fault this time."

"Okay," I relented. "Well, that would probably be a first, but I am glad to hear it."

I wasn't sure if that was the truth, or Sol defending his coworker. He and Estrella, who married into my family, got along pretty well despite her flaws. Plus, he was always looking on the bright side and kept things around the shop upbeat. He lived up to his name for sure, which was why it was so shocking that he and Azura had started dating.

"Do you need any help with anything?" Sol offered. "I feel like I should be doing something."

"No, you just man the counter and eat your sundaes. I'm going to go talk to Azura and pick up some jimsonweed for Lilith."

"I was wondering what you were doing here. I could have sworn you said you'd be out all day unless there was an emergency."

"If it's not one thing with my family, it's something else," I said with a shrug.

As Sol dug into his brownie mountains, I headed upstairs. At least he'd used a little cold magic to keep the ice cream from melting, and the treats looked as good as they had when he bought them. One of the perks of being a witch. You never had to race against entropy to eat your ice cream.

Upstairs was where we kept all of the items and ingredients we didn't want the tourists getting their hands on. For witches only. There was even a sign that said it, but it was written in magic ink, so only witches could see it. Kinda pointless except that it was also warded. For reasons they would never understand, the normies would just avoid the upstairs area of the shop like the plague.

Estrella wasn't upstairs, so I could only assume she was in the breakroom having coffee. She did that a lot, but if a customer was ticked off, it was probably better if she stayed out of sight. Especially when that customer was a witch. The last thing I needed was a magical showdown in my shop with a festival revving up outside. She could just sip her coffee, which she made in the breakroom instead of buying from the Brew Station, and stay out of sight until the unhappy customer was gone.

Since I knew where everything was, it didn't take me more than a few seconds to find what I needed. We had a whole section of shelves dedicated to poison plants. We had them dried and then also seeds for those interested in a little gardening. Occasionally, I stocked fresh cuttings, but those were hard to come by. Any witch growing her own poison plants had use for them and most likely didn't want to sell. And when they did, it was expensive. Even with the higher prices, any fresh poison herbs disappeared off the shelves as soon as I stocked them. So, Lilith would have to make do with dried.

I grabbed two bags of dehydrated jimsonweed as Azura's customer thanked her for all the help. At least one of my employees had made a good impression.

Maybe the grumpy witch had found a kindred spirit in Azura because she looked like she was having the worst day imaginable. And Azura was someone who suffered from permanent resting witch face.

A few seconds after the customer headed downstairs to check out, Azura looked like she intended to follow. I called out her name and asked her to hold on for a second. "Azura, I want to talk to you for a second."

I could have sworn as I approached her that she swiped a tear away from her right eye. Of course, by the time I'd crossed the distance between us, she had her resting witch face firmly in place again.

"What's up, boss?" She tried to sound snarky, but I heard a definite quiver in her voice. "Was Estrella complaining about me again?" Azura said with an overly dramatic eye roll. She was trying way too hard to convince me she was her regular, grumpy self.

"Sol said you didn't want to eat the brownie mountain he bought for you, so I was concerned," I said. "Since when do you not like brownies? I know you don't like most things... but chocolate?"

"So what if I didn't want the stupid brownie, ugh," she sniffled and then wiped her eye again. "I would have paid for it myself. He didn't have to buy me anything."

"I don't think that's the issue," I said gently. "It's pretty obvious something is wrong, Azura. He's just worried about you. And frankly, I'm a bit concerned too. This isn't like you at all."

"I know," she said with another sniffle. "It's the worst."

I just stared at her for a second. Something was off. I could almost put my finger on it, but not quite.

"I just wish he'd let it go," she huffed. "He's always got to be so dumb and caring. He needs to let it go and leave me alone."

"Azura, I think he did. It's not like he's following you around pressuring you to tell him what's wrong. He seems to be giving you your space."

"He sent you instead," she retorted. "You think I don't know he sent you? He can't drop anything."

"No, he didn't. He didn't even ask me to talk to you. I just saw him eating two brownie mountain supreme things, and he said you didn't want much of yours. He did tell me that you seemed upset, but I'm your boss. I don't think it was wrong for him to mention it."

"I know," she admitted and pulled a tissue out of her pocket. "I just wish he'd stop being so nice. It's only going to make him dumping me so much more painful. I keep trying to push him away, so he doesn't have to dump me, and he just keeps trying to take care of me. It's insane. How is it possible that someone so wonderful exists? And I managed to completely screw it up."

Okay, now we were getting somewhere. Which was good, because while I didn't want to just ditch Azura while she was in pain, I needed to get back to Lilith.

"Why on earth would he dump you, Azura? You realize that Sol is completely smitten with you and probably was long before the two of you started dating. He's trying to take care of you because he probably loves you."

"I'm pregnant," she blurted out.

"Oh."

"Don't say it like that. It's scary when you say it like that," she pleaded.

"I didn't mean to scare you. It's just not what I expected you to say," I replied. "Does Sol know? Because that might also be why he's so insistent on taking care of you… I don't understand."

I had a hard time imagining he did know. If Sol knew, he'd have said something when I was downstairs. He'd be too excited to contain himself not worrying himself silly over a brownie mountain.

"I haven't told him," she confessed before worrying her bottom lip. "We've only been dating a few months. There's no way he's going to be okay with this. It's too soon. We're not ready. He's going to completely freak out, and then it will all be over. What am I going to do? I can't raise a baby on my own, and I can't lose him either. You think he loves me, but I know I love him."

"You're joking, right?" I said, completely deadpan. "Like, you've met Sol, right? You think he's going to dump you because you're having his baby? Or wait… it's not his baby?"

"Yes, it's his. Of course it's his. I would never do anything to hurt Sol."

"Well, yeah. I figured. But I guess it was possible you were already pregnant when you started dating him… I'm sorry, I wasn't trying to insult you."

"It's okay. And no, I wasn't already knocked up when I met him. Before Sol, it had been a long time since I'd even dated anyone."

"Okay, well, you have to tell him, Azura. You're upset. He's upset. But I don't think there's any reason for any of it. He's not going to dump you, Azura."

"You sure?" she asked me hopefully.

"Again, you've met him, right?"

She visibly relaxed. "You're right. I've worked myself up into a tizzy with the horrible stories I keep telling myself. I'll tell him tonight over dinner."

"I think that's a good idea."

"Do you think there are any of those brownie mountains left?" she asked as her stomach growled.

"I'm sure there are."

With that, she hurried off to reclaim her brownie mountain. As I was leaving the store, the two of them were behind the counter eating and chatting. The relief on Sol's face was palpable, and Azura looked like a thousand pounds had been lifted from her shoulders.

"Take two bags of jimsonweed off the inventory when you're done," I said to Sol. "And you guys have a great day."

Chapter Two

As soon as I pulled into Lilith's driveway, something felt off. Meri had dozed off on the short ride back, but he raised his head and sniffed the air. In a flash, he stood up. The hair on his hackles raised, and he let out a low warning snarl.

"What is it?" I asked, but I was already pulling myself out of the car.

Meri darted past me to the front door, and I walked around the flagstone path to avoid falling during what I could already tell was an emergency. As soon as I hit the bottom step, Meri disappeared.

At first, I thought he'd vanished into thin air, but then I realized Lilith's front door was open. Meri had gone inside ahead of me and worry for him made my heart clench like a vice in my chest.

"He's fine," I reminded myself, but suddenly, nothing felt fine.

"Lilith?" I called out as I pushed the front door further open. "Meri?"

Meri came running at me from deeper inside the house. "Go back outside," he said in a voice devoid of any humor.

"What? No. What's going on?" I felt my chest clench again. "Lilith!"

I called out to her several times as panic rose like acid into my throat. I still had no reason to be terrified, but I was. There was something outside of me fueling my fear. It's like that tone produced from thunderstorms that they pump into movies. You can't actually hear it, but it activates your panic to let you know when you should be afraid.

A cover for bad writing… except that I wasn't in a movie. No one was writing this story.

Something was wrong with my Auntie Lilith, and Meri was trying to keep me from her. I turned a skeptical eye to him.

"Get out of my way, cat," I said as I stepped over him.

"Kinsley! No. You don't need to see this," he said and trailed after me.

Meri had never given me a reason to distrust him, but in that moment, everything felt upside down. The world had shattered into a million little puzzle pieces, and I didn't know how to fit them back together.

And then I found her.

Lilith was on her back in the kitchen. A glass of what looked to be soda had fallen on the tile floor. It didn't shatter, but the liquid fanned out to one side.

I fell to my knees and tried to shake her. Someone was screaming her name, and it took Meri rubbing against my left thigh to make me realize it was me.

"She's gone," he said as I continued to shake her.

"She's not. She can't be."

I realized I had to calm down, though. I closed my eyes and searched inside her for the light. Her life light. It had to be there. I couldn't see or feel her ghost anywhere, so she had to be in there somewhere.

But there was nothing. Not even a flicker. Lilith was gone, and as gone as she was, it had to have happened right after I left.

After practically leaping to my feet, I hurried into the dining room. Lilith didn't have a crystal ball on the table, but I was able to easily locate one in one of her many china hutches, which were not filled with china…

"What are you doing?" Meri asked as he jumped onto the table and settled onto a piece of parchment.

"I'm going to contact her," I said and started lighting the candles that had gone out.

"You're doing a séance to reach Lilith?" Meri seemed sincere.

The worried edge to his voice told me he didn't think it was the best idea. But it was the only idea I had, and I felt like if I didn't do something, I would spin out into the universe.

"Kinsley, if Lilith wanted to contact you, she would," he said gently. "You wouldn't need to do this."

"No!" I said and lit the last candle. "If I can reach out and grab her spirit, I can put it back."

"You need to call Thorn," was his reply.

"Murdered…" the word dripped off my lips like something I hadn't been able to fully spit out. "But how?"

"I don't know, Kinsley. But someone able to kill a witch has been here recently."

"It's impossible. How could anyone kill Lilith?" But what was I saying? The only other alternative was that she'd done it to herself… "What if it was just a heart attack? If it was a widow-maker, she would have gone unconscious immediately. She wouldn't have had time to heal herself. We can bring her back."

"Kinsley, there was something wrong with her mouth."

I was about to reply, but I realized he was right. Black foam at the corner of her mouth. It wasn't just where she'd coughed up some soda.

He was right.

"Still, I can bring her back. If I can reach out to her spirit, I can. I don't know… shove it back into her body. Surely, she's got a spell like that around here. It was her specialty. Get off that parchment. I need some necromancy."

"First of all, rude," Meri snarked. "I know you're upset but there's no reason to be impolite."

I was about to snap at him, but something about his typical sass grounded me. It brought me back to the moment. Meri's snark walked me back from the ledge.

"I have to try," I whispered because I wasn't quite willing to give up even if I knew I was being a little unhinged. "If I can bring her spirit back to her body and heal the damage…"

"All right," Meri relented. "Five minutes and then you call stick-in-the-mud. If her spirit is here, it's got to be close. If she's here, it shouldn't take much."

I took a deep breath.

So deep that I nearly blew a candle out, but Meri flicked his tail, and it stayed lit. "Lilith," I called out once I was sure the séance circle would stay intact.

"There's nothing," Meri insisted. "There aren't even any lost souls or demons hanging around."

"Don't you think that's weird?" I pondered aloud even though I was supposed to be talking to Lilith and not Meri.

"I think it just means you're bad at this."

"Oh, hush, Meri. What I mean is don't you think it's weird because there aren't any ghosts, demons, or ghouls around here? At Lilith's house? She was always meddling with ghosts and necromancy. She has to have angered more dead people than the entire population of Coventry. And yet, nothing."

"I imagine with as many ghosts as she did tick off, this place is probably heavily warded for protection."

"You're right!" I said with a snap of my fingers. "Do you think that's why she's not here either?"

"Like she's being kept away by her own wards?" Meri asked. "That would be pretty dumb."

"It's not like she anticipated dying in her own house. How would she know?"

"Well, then we just remove the wards, right? And she'll pop right up when we call," Meri snarked.

"Good plan except the little matter of trying to break a dead witch's spell," I retorted.

"Is something starting to smell?" Meri asked as he sniffed the air.

"Oh, stop it," I said. "Don't be a jerk. This is Lilith we're talking about."

"No, I'm not messing with you. Something smells like… broccoli butt."

"Like when you microwave broccoli?" I asked because fresh cooked broccoli really did smell like a butt.

"Yeah, like that. But like sulfur."

"Broccoli does have sulfur in it. That's why it smells. But that would be a demon. Like you just pointed out, there can't be a demon here."

"And you can't do a séance because of the wards, so how about you just call Thorn."

My shoulders slumped. He was right. But maybe not…

"Maybe I should just handle this," I said. "Like with the vampires… is there anything the sheriff's department can even do? This should be coven business."

"Kinsley, no," Meri's voice full of warning. "You know you can't do that. There's no way you can keep Lilith's death from Thorn. He's going to know, and he'll be upset if he has to go around you to investigate a murder. You could get him in trouble. We're probably interfering now."

"Since when do you care?"

"Kinsley, you're not thinking straight. You have to at least report it. We both know that it will most likely be you, Brighton, and the Aunties who... sort this out, but you have to report it."

"I could just call an ambulance," I retorted. "I could call an ambulance and then clean up the poison before they get here. It had to be poison, right? But that doesn't matter. The rest of the world will assume she had a heart attack or stroke. She's, like, a hundred years old."

"Kinsley, go outside," Meri commanded.

"What?"

"You are losing it, and I want you to go out on the porch and take a few deep breaths of fresh air. Let the sun shine on your skin."

"What? You're the one who sounds crazy now," I said, but I turned around and looked at the front door.

"Go," Meri commanded again. "Just get some air and if you still want to do these crazy schemes after, I'll help you."

"You have to help me anyway," I responded.

"I have to HELP you, Kinsley. I have to do what is best for you, and right now, I don't believe that covering up Lilith's murder is what's best for you. Since I can't hurt you, I can't assist you with it."

"You're the worst," I said with a sniffle.

I suddenly realized how heavy the air around me felt. I had been in somewhat of a daze, and just looking at the front door reminded me that there was a whole world outside it. There was fresh, clean air and warm sunshine.

And suddenly, I wanted it bad. I needed it to fill my lungs with air not tinged in thick sage smoke and sadness… and death.

"I'm going to go outside," I said over my shoulder as I headed toward the door.

Meri, of course, stayed right behind me. He darted out the front door as soon as I opened it and hopped up into one of Lilith's black metal outdoor chairs.

"Maybe you should sit," Meri said and looked over at the other chair.

"No thanks," I descended the front steps and stood in the middle of the front lawn.

If I'd stayed on the front porch, I would have been in the shade, and Meri was right. I needed the sun on my face. I kicked off my shoes too, so I could feel the blades of grass between my toes.

So, I just stood there for a moment, with my eyes closed, taking in all the sensations that weren't overwhelming, suffocating grief. As the sun warmed my skin, it chased away something dark. I felt it evaporate out of my pores as the light cleansed me.

Within minutes, the paranoid panic that had gripped me in the house had dissipated. I felt like I could think straight again.

Meri was right. I would handle whoever had killed Lilith, but I needed to call Thorn. Not because I feared the human authorities.

If it were ever discovered, my lack of reporting the murder could be buried under a mountain of confusing paperwork. We'd had to do it before for other cases where there had been no earthly explanation or resolution.

No, I needed to call Thorn because I needed him. I needed his strong arms around me, and his steadfast gaze fixed on mine as he told me everything would be all right. Because I knew him so well that I already knew how he would act and the things he would say.

And I needed his strength.

So, I took out my phone and dialed. As I waited for him to pick up, Meri walked in little circles around my legs. He rubbed his face against my shin reassuringly and then sat at my feet.

Because he knew that I would wait right there in that spot for Thorn. I couldn't go back into the house and look at her again.

And I was wrong. I didn't stand there in that spot. As soon as I hung up the phone and thought of Lilith lying there on her kitchen floor, I dropped to my knees. Uncontrollable sobs racked my body as I tried to breathe.

Meri was there beside me the whole time. I could feel his furry body pressed against the side of my thigh. The scent of the grass filled my nose, and that earthly scent combined with the reassurance of soft fur was the only thing that kept me from losing my mind.

After a few minutes of sobs so intense that I would have sworn my body could shatter into a million little pieces with a stiff breeze, I vaguely heard a car pull up. A door slam shut. Someone calling my name.

And then he was there. I thought that I would have to beg him not to pull me to my feet. I wasn't sure my legs would work, and I didn't have the oxygen to test them out.

But Thorn just knelt beside me in the grass. He held me right there where I was. Even as other cars arrived and the deputies went about their business, Thorn stayed right there with me in my spot on Lilith's front lawn.

All I could do was weep and try to suck in gasping breaths between sobs. He smoothed my hair and handed me tissues. Because Thorn kept a box in his cruiser for the arrestees who cried or for loved ones who lost someone at accident scenes.

Eventually, another car pulled up. I could tell right away that it wasn't a sheriff's cruiser. No sooner had two doors slammed shut, than I could feel my mom and dad.

I finally looked up. "You didn't bring the girls, right?" I said between sobs.

"Of course not," Mom said.

And she did pull me to my feet, but amazingly, my legs worked. Before I could think too hard about it, I was encircled in a hug with my mom, dad, and Thorn. Meri was still at my feet. Well, he was between my feet. In my mind's eye, I could see his silky black fur pressed against both of my legs.

But I broke the hug. Just a little. And just long enough to reach down and pull Meri up into my arms. He squirmed a little as my family's embrace tightened, because he was still Meri after all, but he also purred.

He hummed with magical energy that resonated with my heartbeat. It slowed my skyrocketing pulse.

"She's gone," I whispered, and at first, I wasn't sure if anybody even heard me. "She's gone," I said again.

There was one last squeeze, and our little circle broke apart. When it did, a deputy approached. No, not a deputy, I realized as I wiped the tears out of my eyes. It was Jeremy.

"I need to take her statement," he tried to say it to Thorn under his breath, but I heard.

"Not now," Thorn replied. "They need a few minutes."

"No, I can do it," I protested. "I want to get it over with so we can…"

"What is it?" Thorn asked as he took my hand.

"So we can what? I don't know what we're supposed to do next," I said and felt the hysteria rising in my gut.

Thorn squeezed my hand again. "It's okay. We'll get through this."

"You're dang right we will," Mom said as she started for Lilith's front door.

"Brighton, where are you going?" Jeremy asked as Thorn let go of my hand.

Both of them attempted to follow my mother as she stomped up the front steps. Dad gave me a shrug, but then he started to follow behind them. He stayed back, though. After all their years of marriage, he'd learned to stay out of her way.

"I'll keep an eye on her," Dad said over his shoulder. "Unless…"

"I'm okay," I lied. "Just make sure they don't arrest her."

"I need to see the body!" Mom hollered from just inside Lilith's front door.

"You better go knock her out or something," I said to Meri.

"I need to stay here with you," he protested.

"She's not taking this well," I said with a sigh. "What I really need is for her to not force Thorn to arrest her today."

"Fine," Meri said and trotted off.

That left me standing alone in Lilith's front yard. I kicked the edge of one of the flagstone pavers gently with my toe. The repetitive motion kept my mind from spiraling. I had to figure out how I was going to break the news to Laney and Hekate. Laney would take it hard. Hekate would unleash fury.

Not unlike my mother whose yelling broke into my thoughts. "Cat! I know you can't die, but if you try that again, I'll skin you alive!"

I started for the front door, but before I even got up the first step, Meri came streaking out of the house. He bounded across the front lawn and took off down the street.

Seconds later, my mother emerged from the house. She chased him down the road but only made it a couple hundred feet before she turned around to face me.

"Don't you do that again. I know you put him up to that!" she said as she marched back over to me.

"Mama," I pleaded. "You've got to calm down. You're losing it, and we need you to hold it together."

She softened for a second. Just long enough to wipe one of my tears away with her thumb. Then her face set again like hard steel, and I saw the fire reignite behind her eyes.

"This is not a time for tears and sadness," she choked on the words. "We'll have that soon enough. Right now, we have to figure out who killed her. We have to figure it out now while the trail is still warm."

I heard a shuffle in the grass behind me. I hadn't realized that Thorn, Jeremy, and my dad had followed her back out.

Dad spoke first. "Brighton, sweetie, I'm taking you home."

"The hell you are!" She started to get really mad again.

"I am taking you home," he said with all the love and patience in the world. "You're in shock. You need some tea and some time to think. You're no good to anyone like this, and I refuse to let this all fall on Kinsley's shoulders."

Mom looked like she was ready to unleash the fire of a thousand suns on him, but then she looked at me again. "Okay, but I want to stay here with Kinsley."

"I've got to give a statement, Mom. You go home and have some tea. I'll come over when I'm done here, and we'll figure out what to do next." And just like that, I got myself together.

She nodded and then hugged me tight one more time. "I'm sorry."

"You don't have to be sorry. I'm angry too. I don't know… but we'll figure this out."

Dad took Mom to the car and helped her in. Once she was secure, he walked quickly back over to me. "I can drop her off and come back. I feel so bad leaving you like this."

"I'm not alone," I answered. "Thorn's here, and I'm sure once the danger of being skinned is gone, Meri will be back."

"Okay," he said and kissed my cheek. "If you need me, call."

"I will, but I'm sure I'll be fine. I'll give my statement, and then I'll be right over."

He left, and after my parents' car had pulled away, I turned my attention back to Thorn and Jeremy. Both of them stood there waiting patiently.

"Are you okay?" Thorn asked. "I can delay the statement. You could take the rest of the day and then come in tomorrow. It doesn't have to be right now."

"No, it's better if it is. I want to do it while everything is fresh," and while I was still partially numb. "I want to get it over with."

Thorn nodded. "Jeremy is going to take your statement. I shouldn't because of my connection to you and Lilith."

"I figured," I said.

"I'm going to go check with the crime scene techs," Thorn said, and that was the first time I realized they'd arrived.

"Okay."

I watched Thorn walk into the house. When he was gone, I turned and offered Jeremy a soft smile.

"You really don't have to do this right now," Jeremy reassured me. "I'm sorry I even said anything about it before."

"There's too much to do," I said, but Jeremy looked confused. "There's too much to do for me to wait. I'm going to have to plan the funeral plus there are going to be issues with the coven. I can't take time tomorrow to do it, so let's do it now."

"Issues with the coven?" Jeremy's eyebrow shot up.

"You saw how upset my mother got. I hope she's the only one who loses it like that, but I just don't know.

Lilith is… was a coven elder. She was important to everyone. To the entire town even. I can't imagine this is going to go over well. The damage control alone is going to be a full-time job for a few days. Plus, you have to understand, her funeral isn't going to be a regular service. People are going to come from all over. I mean a lot of them are probably already here for the food festival. I'm going to have to make sure the funeral is after it's over. So many of those people will stay. It's probably going to be chaos."

Jeremy sighed. "Okay, well, then let's just start with your statement."

"I got here to take her to the festival, and she sent me out on an errand…" I began before telling him about the rest of the morning.

Chapter Three

I left Lilith's house as soon as I'd given my statement.
By the time I arrived at my parents' house, there were
already a dozen cars parked in their driveway and up
and down their street.

I parked a block over and started the short walk back
to their house. Aside from everything that happened,
it was a lovely day. The sun was shining, and birds
were singing. But as I got halfway there, a cold breeze
blew stiffly through my jersey dress.

Since I didn't have a cardigan, I wrapped my arms
around my middle as best I could. A strange, sweet
smell drifted on that gentle wind, and I noticed some
fat, gray clouds roll in.

My parents' front door was open with just the screen
door between their house and the rest of the world. I
let myself in and put my hand back to keep it from
banging shut.

There was a general buzz of activity and hushed
voices that came to a screeching halt when I walked
in. I turned to look into the living room where I saw
my dad sitting with Auntie Amelda, his grandmother,
on their sofa. On the other side of my great-
grandmother was someone I rarely saw. Annika, dad's

cousin, and Amelda's other favorite grandchild, sat close by holding the old woman's hand.

We rarely saw Annika. She'd become estranged from the family due to a plethora of issues. Mostly to do with her husband's mental health concerns. Speaking of Gunther, he sat in a chair near the sofa staring at his thumbs.

Annika wasn't particularly close to Lilith, but when she was younger, she'd been inseparable from my father, and as I'd said before, she was one of Amelda's favorite grandchildren. So of course, she'd rushed to Amelda's side. There was nothing like a death in the family to finally bring people back together.

My mother wasn't in the room, and I could feel tension in the air. Gunner's illness wasn't the only thing that had estranged Annika from the family. She'd also become jealous of my mom's relationship with my dad.

Not because of any romantic feelings, they were related after all, but as I'd said, until my mother showed up in Coventry, Dad and Annika had been inseparable best friends. For a long time, Mom and Annika were best friends too.

And then one day they weren't. One day, Annika couldn't stand that my mom and dad were best friends too. People got weird about things you'd never expect.

At least, that's what I'd always assumed. If there was more to the story, Mom and Dad had kept it from me. And that moment wasn't the time to dive down that rabbit hole.

"Can I get you anything, Auntie Amelda?" Was the first thing I could think to say.

It wasn't even my house, but I felt the need to play hostess. Possibly so Mom could stay in the other room until she was ready to deal with Annika and Gunner.

"Your mom is making her some tea," Dad said softly. "Why don't you go see if you can help her."

"Belladonna," Amelda added.

"No, Grandma," Annika said and patted Amelda's hand.

Amelda yanked her hand away from Annika that it made her wince. "Don't presume to come back here after all this time and tell me what to do."

Dad flashed Annika a pained look, but I knew he was hurt by Annika's estrangement too. He looked at me and pressed his lips into a line.

It was my decision, but I would never presume to tell Amelda what to do. Especially not at such a time. Not when she had just lost one of her favorite sisters. She was a very old woman, but that didn't mean she should be treated like a child.

I just nodded at Dad and headed into the kitchen. If Amelda wanted a little bit of belladonna in her tea, then I'd give her some. She was a strong witch, and not even a massive dose of nightshade would kill her, but I'd still take it easy. Either way, I wasn't going to argue with Annika about it.

"Where are you going?" I heard Annika say as I walked into the kitchen.

My eyes met my mom's, and we heard the front door closed. I figured Gunner must have gone outside for some reason. He'd looked wildly uncomfortable when I'd been in the living room before.

"Do you have Amelda's tea?" I asked. "She wants some belladonna added. Annika didn't want her to have it, so probably go easy."

"I don't give a rat's patoot what Annika wants," Mom said viciously.

"Mom, please don't. I know things are strained with you guys, but not today, okay? I'll finish making the tea and take it in there, though. You don't have to."

"Thanks," Mom said and handed me a delicate china teacup on a white saucer. "I think I'm going to make some lunch."

"You sure you don't want me to order something? I could even go pick it up, or I'll spring for the delivery fees."

"Thanks, sweetie, but that's okay. Cooking will give me something to do."

"Okay."

"Oh, wait, there is something you can do."

"Anything," I replied.

"I have coffee and tea, but I wasn't prepared for this. I don't have nearly enough cold drinks for the amount of witches who are probably going to pass through this house today."

"I will run to Mann's and clean them out of Coke, Diet Coke, and anything else?"

"Maybe some iced tea… no, wait, I can make that. Well, either some lemons or some bottled lemonade."

"You got it," I said. "Are you sure you don't want me to get any food?"

"I'm going to cook, but if you want to go to the deli counter and get some fried chicken and those crispy potato wedges, that would be good. I'm not sure if I can feed everybody," she said with a deep sigh.

"You don't have to, Mom. If you want to cook, go ahead. But I'll get the chicken, potatoes, and some cold salads too."

"Thank you so much," Mom replied. "I know shopping is probably the last thing you want to be doing right now."

"Gives me something to do," I said. "Kind of like you and cooking. If I'm busy, I can't sit around being sad."

"Well, when you get back, you can help me bake a cake. And we should do a tray of those funeral potatoes too."

"We can do that."

I hugged her, but not long enough to make us both start crying again, and then headed out. I told Dad, and everyone else gathered in the living room, that I was headed out to get cold drinks.

For a moment, I thought Dad was going to offer to go, but Amelda grabbed his hand and sniffled. So, I set out without him.

I was sure everyone already knew what was going on, but I sent Viv a text apologizing for not stopping by that morning like I'd planned. Then I put my phone in my purse and headed to Mann's for groceries.

I avoided the town square because it was blocked off for the festival. When I got to the grocery store, it was a ghost town. That wasn't exactly shocking considering there was a food festival going on in town.

So, I parked close, not something I would normally do but I was in a hurry and headed inside. There was no line at the deli counter, and the young woman working was relieved that I was there to buy so much food.

"I thought we were going to end up having to throw all of this out," she said as she put the potato wedges into white boxes. "I don't know why we didn't just hold off on making this food, but it's what we do every day. The manager said to just proceed as normal."

"I guess it's a good thing you did," I said with a half-smile.

"You're right. It is a good thing I did. Can I get you anything else?"

"How many pounds of cold salads do those bowls hold?" I asked as I pointed to the display.

"I think I put about five pounds of each out at a time," she said.

"Okay, well, give me all your potato, deviled egg and potato, broccoli, pasta, and macaroni salads. Oh, and the coleslaw. Can't forget the coleslaw."

"You want biscuits?" she asked.

"That's an excellent idea."

I waited as she put the cold salads I ordered into massive plastic tubs. Only one other customer came into the grocery store while I waited, and she quickly bought a bag of flour and a huge bag of what looked like walnuts. Probably someone who needed more supplies for the festival.

When my order was ready, the girl brough the tubs around the counter instead of trying to hand them over the top. She helped me stack them in the cart.

"I'm sorry for your loss," she said before I could wheel away.

"Oh, thank you," I said. "Do I know you?"

"Not really. I mean, I eat at your donut shop as much as I can. So, I thought I recognized you. And when you started buying all this food, I figured it was for…"

"Yeah. We've got a lot of family to feed today."

"Well, if you need anything for after the actual funeral, just call me. My name's Bethany. I can have a large order ready for you in the walk-in cooler. That way you don't have to come in and wait like this."

"I appreciate that," I said. "I hadn't even gotten to the planning part yet."

"Well, anything I can do to make it easier for you."

"Thank you so much," I said. "I hope you have a good rest of your day."

She just nodded at me and I pushed my cart away. It was heavy, but I wrangled it over to the soda aisle. I knew I'd probably have to use a little magic to get it up to the checkouts after I filled it with soda.

I really did clean the store out of Coke and Diet Coke. If they'd had more, I probably would have built a pyramid of it in the cart. Once I found the bottles of lemonade, I added a few of those too.

If we needed any more than what I'd gotten, I'd just have to come back. Or go to the gas station since I already had all of the soda.

Fortunately, there was no one at the checkout to grumble and complain about my huge haul. Even the checkout girl seemed glad to have something to do.

"Pretty dead in here, huh?" she asked and then turned bright red. "I'm so sorry. I mean… I'm sorry for your loss. I didn't mean to say it that way."

"You don't need to apologize," I said and supposed I'd have to get used to it. People were already going to know about Lilith's passing, and many of them would make a big deal about it. And who was I to say they shouldn't? "It's a common phrase, and yes, it is very quiet today. Probably because of the food festival."

"I'm planning on going after work," she said as she hauled my giant tubs of salads over the scanner. "I love your donuts. I hope there are some of the special ones left."

"I'm sure there will be. I can count on my employees," I said and then stared out the store's front windows. Normally, I would love talking to a happy customer, but I suddenly felt exhausted by conversation.

The checkout girl took the hint and finished my order quietly. I thanked her before pushing my cart out of the store.

I was about halfway to my car when I saw a woman making a beeline for me across the parking lot. She looked to be about middle-aged, and the closer she got, the easier it was to tell she was furious.

Great.

Just what I needed.

But I was at least a little bit curious to know why the woman looked like she wanted to go gladiator on me in a grocery store parking lot. Maybe she really didn't like the special festival donuts.

I thought they were cute. Cake donuts with deep purple frosting and little white candy ghosts. Some of them had witch hats and cauldrons too.

"Excuse me!" she said once she was a few feet from me.

"Can I help you?" I asked as I hoisted a tub of macaroni salad into the trunk of my car.

"I think you can," she practically spat at me.

I looked her over if for no other reason than to size her up. She had her dishwater blonde hair, obviously a dye job because her roots were gray, tied back in a low ponytail. Her sweatpants were clean, but not new, and she'd thrown a beige cable-knit cardigan over a faded floral graphic tee.

"Oh, good. That's what I wanted most today. To help someone who was rude to me in a grocery store parking lot on the day my beloved Auntie died," I said back completely deadpan.

"You're just like her," the woman hissed and then scuffed her black Croc over the asphalt like a bull getting ready to charge.

She didn't though. It appeared to be more of a discharge of nervous tension than an overt sign of aggression.

"Just like who?" I asked the question, but I had a feeling I already knew who she was talking about.

"That Lilith. She's nothing but a snake in the grass!"

"Ma'am, Lilith died today. And I'm not in the mood to deal with some stranger belittling her in a parking lot."

"Well, then you can just pay me the money she owes me, and I'll be on my way."

"Excuse me?"

"She owes me money, and now that she's dead, I'll never get it. So, you can pay me, and I'll be on my way."

"Really, ma'am? On the day she died? You're going to accost me at my car and demand money?"

"We're all better off without her anyway," the woman snarled.

And I couldn't believe it. This woman had to know who we were, right? And she was pulling this crap now? When I was in the kind of mental state where I would happily put this miserable... woman in a jar.

"You need to stop before something bad happens," I said. "I'm not in the mood today."

"Like I said, pay me what she owes me, and you'll never have to deal with me again."

"First of all, what's your name?" I demanded.

"Charity Lubbox," she said as if I should already know that.

"Okay, Charity. Since you don't have the good sense to walk away and handle this at a more appropriate time, why don't you tell me why you believe Lilith owes you money?"

"It's not that I believe anything," Charity snapped. "She did owe me money, and now you do. Her debts pass down to her next of kin, and I happened to see you here putting all that party food in your car. If you can afford all that, you can afford to pay me my money. It's a thousand dollars. I'll take cash."

"Do I look like I keep a thousand dollars in cash on me?" I asked in disbelief. "Do you ever have that much cash on you?"

Charity looked at my cart and trunk full of groceries and shook her head. "That stuff does look expensive."

"I didn't say I don't have any money. I said I don't carry that much cash around on me. Who does?"

"We could go to an ATM. I could wait in your car at the bank."

"Whoa, wait a minute. First of all, no. That's how people get robbed. Also, you still haven't told me why you think Lilith owes you a thousand dollars."

Charity let out an exaggerated sigh and rolled her eyes again. "I bought a potion from her. Well, more of an elixir, she called it. She said it would cure my husband's cheating."

"That doesn't sound like something anyone in my family would sell," I said. "And you expect me to believe you paid a thousand dollars for it."

"Cut the crap, lady. I know what you are. I'm a half-witch myself."

More like a halfwit, I thought.

"So why didn't you just make this elixir for yourself?" I said. "And that sounds dangerously like a love spell. Which no one in my family would do or sell."

"Well, I asked her for the potion. She took half the money up front because the ingredients were supposedly expensive. Lilith made the potion and handed it over when I paid the other half."

"And?" I pressed.

"And I gave it to my husband," Charity said with a shrug.

"And?" I lost the battle to keep the annoyed edge from my voice. Not only was the conversation going nowhere, but I needed to get the deli salads back to my mom's house and stacked into her refrigerators before they went bad.

"And he filed for divorce the same day. I put it in his morning coffee, and by the time he was supposed to come home from work, there was a process server on my front porch."

I thought it over for a moment. "Sounds like the potion worked to me," I finally said.

"What?!" she shrieked. "What are you talking about, you crazy witch! There is something wrong with all of you. Nothing but a bunch of no-good scammers! How could you possibly think the potion worked? That potion… or elixir… whatever you want to call it, it didn't save my marriage! He divorced me!"

"You didn't ask Lilith for a potion to save your marriage, Charity. And if you had, she would have told you no. What you asked for was a potion to make him stop cheating. He can't cheat on you if you're not married."

"No," she said it as a soft whisper hiss.

"Yes," I replied. "He divorced you right away. Therefore, he's not cheating on you anymore. The potion worked. So, nobody owes you anything."

"You're a liar."

"I'm not a liar. Everything I just said is the truth. I'm sorry that your marriage ended in divorce, but it sounds to me like it was for the best. Lilith helped you."

"If she wasn't dead, I would..."

"You would what?" I squared my shoulders. If this crazy chick wanted a fight, well, I found myself in the mood for a little black magic. I'd learned a thing or two from Lilith over the years.

"I'll get you," she said, but then turned and walked quickly away.

I didn't go after her. There was no point. She was just a sad woman who was lashing out because she'd lost her marriage. Plus, my fried chicken was getting cold.

Chapter Four

Lilith's funeral was two days later. Thankfully, so many witches had pitched in to help that my mother and I barely had to lift a finger. Amelda stayed at my Mom's house for a couple of days, but the day of the funeral, she went home to get ready.

My mother and father planned to pick her up on the way to the funeral home. The only problem that I encountered on the day of the service was that Laney didn't want to go.

I had to step in to stop a physical fight between Hekate and her sister when my younger daughter heard Laney say she didn't want to go. "How dare you!" Hekate hissed in a rage I'd never expected from a child so young.

Lilith's death hit her hard, and it just kept hitting.

"It's okay," I said to both of them. "Funerals aren't for everyone, and Laney doesn't need to go to remember or honor Lilith."

Relief washed over Laney's face, but Hekate crossed her arms defiantly over her chest. "She's just being a baby."

"You're not being fair," I said to Hekate. "I know you're hurting, but you can't take it out on your sister.

Why don't you go downstairs and see if your dad needs help with anything before we leave?"

"Fine," she said and stomped off.

"I'm not a baby," Laney protested as soon as her sister was gone.

"I know," I said and pulled her in for a hug. "She'll understand someday."

"So I can stay home? With Bonkers?"

"I don't know if I can just leave you here. You are only eight," I said and bit my bottom lip.

The problem was that everyone we knew was going to the funeral. I couldn't even drop her off at the shop or my store because I'd closed them for the day.

"I can take care of myself. I'm only eight, but I'm a witch."

She was right, but I still didn't feel right leaving an eight-year-old by herself. Especially not when everyone we knew would be at the funeral. Everyone would have their phones turned off.

"There's a really nice garden outside of the funeral home. You don't have to come inside, but I think you and Bonkers should hang out there. At least then, you'll be close."

She thought it over. "Okay," she relented. "Is there a pond or a fountain in the garden?"

"There are both," I said.

That seemed to satisfy her, so she ran off to see if Thorn needed any help with anything. I didn't hear a fight start between her and Hekate again, so I finished getting ready.

When I got downstairs, Thorn and the girls were waiting patiently on the sofa. Meri must have been in the kitchen, but as soon as I was by the front door, he came running into the living room.

We all loaded into the car, and the ride over to the funeral home was a quiet and somber one. Not even Meri had anything to say, but I figured Lilith would have liked it if he would let some snark fly.

She wouldn't have liked all of the moping and sadness. But I couldn't help how I felt. And how I felt was that a big part of me had been ripped away.

I was close with most of my family, but I hadn't realized how close Lilith and I had grown over the years until she was gone. I was lamenting the fact that I couldn't even contact her spirit, and how unfair that was, when we pulled into the funeral home parking lot.

We had to take a space that was at the end of the lot. Not that it was a huge parking area. The small-town funeral home wasn't used to having to accommodate such huge services.

The portion taking place at the funeral parlor was family only, but it was still overrun with witches. The graveside service would be open to anyone, and I couldn't imagine the chaos that could ensue.

Lilith would have loved it, which is why I allowed it. Otherwise, I would have kept the entire shebang as intimate, and coven only, as I could.

I walked Laney through the gates of the solace garden. Thorn took Hekate inside. I thought it was best that we just separate them then. Hekate was on edge already, and I didn't want to give her the opportunity to start another fight with her sister.

After leaving Laney in the garden with some cousins who also didn't want to go in, I headed inside. All in all, the service was very sedate… and dare I say boring. I felt a tinge of guilt because it wouldn't be what she wanted.

In my mind, as we were getting back into the car to drive into the cemetery, I kept picturing the funerals in New Orleans with parades and jazz musicians. That was something Lilith could have gotten behind, but it wasn't the type of service available in Coventry.

As we took our seats around her grave, there was no way we were putting Lilith in the family crypt, a thought flitted into my mind like a butterfly landing on a flower.

Lilith's house was heavily warded. Like, super-duper heavily warded.

No one could have broken in and poisoned her Diet Coke. Whoever was in her house, whoever had done this to her, she had to let them in. She had to have trusted them enough to let them walk around freely. Enough so that they could have casually gotten into her refrigerator.

Who did that sound like?

It sounded like family. I realized that I was completely surrounded by hundreds of potential suspects. The graveyard was packed with them, and more witches just kept coming.

So many that they were now standing around the chairs and gravesite. There weren't enough metal folding chairs in Coventry to accommodate the funeral-goers who kept arriving.

The thought was overwhelming. Of the hundreds of people around me, my family and coven, one of them had killed Lilith. How would I figure it out?

I shook my head. It seemed impossible. Not solving the murder, but that someone in the coven would murder an Auntie. They were terribly powerful but also beloved. Who would do such a thing? And why?

The why would come when I figured out the who. I'd already put down a challenge to my power and banished a bunch of young witches who'd severely threatened my authority.

Who would have risked killing Lilith? I looked around the crowd.

While I wasn't sure what I was looking for, the family that were sobbing and holding each other up weren't it. I saw a couple of groups laughing, so I excused myself and wandered over to them.

We were seated in the front row, and Hekate sat stone stiff in her chair, refusing to take her eyes off the casket. Thorn patted me on the back as I excused myself. His way of letting me know he'd handle the girls and I should do what I needed to do.

I looked off to my left and saw Laney seated under a tree reading a book to one of her dolls with Bonkers at her side. She was close enough that everyone could keep an eye on her but far enough that she didn't have to be involved in the funeral.

Unfortunately, or fortunately depending on how you look at it, the people telling jokes and laughing as softly as they could were just telling stories about Lilith's life and shenanigans. Some people laughed at funerals. It was how they handled their grief, and Lilith would have approved.

I did too. At least some people weren't sitting around bawling in a way that would have drawn Lilith's ire… if it wasn't her funeral.

Part of me kept expecting her to show up and start yelling at us. Yelling at me for planning such a gloomy and depressing sendoff.

Where were the balloons? Where were the zebras and acrobats? That's the kind of party she would have wanted.

But Lilith was gone, and the service was for those of us left behind. So, there were no zebras or acrobats swinging from trapezes. Though I did get a bit of a chuckle imagining upside-down acrobats lowering her casket into the ground.

"You all right?" Thorn asked as I took my seat.

"Yeah," I said and tried to wipe the smile off my face. "Just imagining acrobats on trapezes hanging upside down to lower Lilith into the ground."

Hekate looked up at me with the first smile I'd seen since I had to tell her about Lilith's passing. "She would have liked that," Hekate said with a giggle.

"She really would have," I said.

"Mommy, one of the people walked up to the casket and said a bad word," Hekate said before leaning against me.

My brows knitted together as I looked at Thorn.

"It's true," he replied. "But I said we could tell you later. I didn't want to bother you with it right now."

"Who was it?" I asked.

"We can really talk about it later," Thorn said. "It's not important right now."

"I think it is," I tried to say it softly without an annoyed edge to my voice.

Thorn let out a deep sigh. The kind he breathed when he didn't agree with me but knew better than to push. "She's over there," he said and pointed at a woman standing next to Auntie Calliope.

"That's Aqua Skeenbauer," I said.

"Is that significant?" Thorn asked.

"She's my cousin. Or she's dad's cousin and my second cousin? I'm not quite sure. There are just too many of us to keep track of…"

"Understandable," Thorn said. "That's why your dad keeps those records."

"Right, but I don't have them memorized. Either way, she's a cousin."

"Is she, like, a problem?"

"Not that I've ever seen, but I guess you just never know. Apparently, Lilith was selling potions on the side."

"You think she might have sold a potion to Aqua?" Thorn asked, and it was his turn to have his brows knitted together.

"Not really, but what I'm saying is that she had a whole life that I didn't really know about."

"Most people do," Thorn replied and then threw his hands up in front of him when I scowled. "Not me. I'm an open book with you, sweetie. I'm just stating from my experience in law enforcement. Most people have compartmentalized lives, and people from one segment know very little about the others."

"I just thought I knew her better."

"Well, selling potions sounds just like Lilith to me," Thorn answered. "And how do you know that?"

So, I told him the story about the woman at the grocery store. I'd been so busy over the last couple of days that I hadn't had a chance to tell him about it.

"That sounds just like her," he confirmed when I was done. "Don't you think?"

"Yeah, I do," I finally admitted.

Before we could talk further, Amelda walked to the front of the crowd and adjusted the microphone the funeral home had set up. Normally, a funeral director or a member of the clergy would lead the service, but in our family's case, our elders were handling it.

I would give a eulogy and lead a comfort spell, but even I had stepped back to let the Aunties run the service. I was the coven leader, but this was their sister.

As the Aunties gave their eulogies and led various spells and incantations, my eyes swept the crowd. I kept getting frustrated because other than Aqua looking annoyed and ready to bolt, I couldn't find anyone else acting abnormally.

I should have figured that, though. If someone in the coven killed her, then they'd been around me long enough to know I'd have my eye out at the funeral.

So, either Aqua was going through some things emotionally that made her lash out, or she was just so full of rage at Lilith that she didn't care. I'd talk to her at some point, but I wouldn't do it at the funeral or right after. That day was not the day to bring more strife into the coven.

When the service was over, and Lilith was in the ground, we all had to leave. I didn't want to go. It was the strangest feeling not wanting to leave her behind, but I knew the body in the ground wasn't Lilith. Lilith was gone somewhere else.

So, I forced myself back to the car as a cemetery employee began covering her grave with a backhoe. We got the girls into the car, and I was just getting ready to get in myself when I heard a commotion coming from the direction of the cemetery gates.

The way everyone was pulled into the cemetery, the last cars in had to be the first cars out. That meant that our car would have to wait until almost everyone was gone to leave.

But no one was moving.

Thorn's face took on his usual 'law enforcement' edge, and he said, "Stay here."

"Oh, no," I said with a shake of my head. "You stay here with the girls. This is my business."

"I'll watch them," Amelda said and indicated with a nod of her chin that Thorn should follow me.

So, we strode past the nearly endless lines of cars. Thorn and I picked up our pace as the sounds of commotion turned into outright screaming.

My heart threatened to beat out of my chest, but Thorn stayed right by my side. He tried at least a couple of times to get ahead of me, to put himself between me and the screaming, but I wouldn't allow it. Eventually he relented and fell back a half step.

When we got to the gates, I couldn't believe my eyes. There was a line of protesters outside the cemetery. They were dressed in all-white clothing, but they held big posterboard signs on long wooden sticks. The posters were very colorful and depicted an array of hellscape scenes.

One of the signs said, "Burn in Hell, Witch!" and I felt my blood begin to boil. But I had to stay calm. I could hear a murmur of fury starting to spread through the crowd of witches behind me, and while I wanted to join them, I could not. I was responsible for my coven's actions, so I had to keep my head on straight.

"Move out of the way," I said after marching right up to the man holding the 'burn in hell' sign.

He was in his fifties with stringy gray hair and a huge steel cross around his neck. Under that was a faded, dingy shirt from some sort of Bible camp. His jeans could have done with a good washing too.

"I don't have to do anything, Satan worshiper," he spat back at me.

"I'm not going to argue with you," I said as flatly as possible. "I'm not here to debate religions. We buried my aunt today, and now I'd like for you to move."

"There's no debate, witch. You and your lot are going to burn."

"Move out of the way," Thorn said and stepped in front of me.

I didn't like it, but I understood why. There was a public safety issue at that point. The protesters were blocking the road, and that made it a law enforcement problem.

"Shut up, warlock. I rebuke you," the man hissed, and that earned him cheers from his fellow protesters.

"I am not a warlock, sir, but what I am is the sheriff. You and your group need to move or I'm going to call in my deputies. You'll all be arrested."

"No, don't," I put my hand on Thorn's arm and pleaded. I wasn't sure why, but I could feel something bad coming. I didn't want his department involved. "I can handle this. We can work it out."

"We have the God-given right to assemble," the man stated. "There's nothing you can do about that."

"You don't have the right to block the road or trap people in the cemetery," Thorn said without missing a beat. "God or otherwise, you need to clear a path immediately."

"You can't put us all in jail!" someone called from the line of protestors.

"God will prevail!" someone else screeched.

The murmur from my fellow witches grew stronger behind me. While I admired their patience in the face of such slanderous defamation, I could tell their good will wore thin. We had just put Lilith in the ground. Nobody had the emotional strength to keep dealing with a gaggle of jerks telling us she was in hell. Or that we were all going to hell, for that matter.

"Please leave," I said and tried to use some of my magical energy to pacify the group.

It worked a little. A couple of them broke off from the line and started walking back to their cars. Probably people who hadn't really wanted to do a funeral protest in the first place...

The rest of them just snickered and jeered.

"Turn them into goats!" someone called out from behind me.

"Put them in a jar!" one of the Aunties called out.

I understood the sentiment, but it didn't help. "Calm down, guys," I said over my shoulder to the witches. "Don't give into them. That's what they want."

"Well, if that's what they want…" Meri said.

Fortunately, the protesters didn't seem to understand it was the huge black cat at my feet that had said the last part.

"See! Nothing but a bunch of devil worshipers!" the ringleader said. "They want to sacrifice us to their dark god!"

I rolled my eyes at him. My patience was so thin, it was about to snap. "We actually just want to go home," I said calmly. "Please move out of the way so we can mourn our loved one."

"No chance, witch!" he howled. "You're going to burn!"

And for a moment, I wondered if they were actually going to try to set us on fire. I sniffed the air and felt reasonably reassured when I didn't smell any gas or kerosene.

Thorn, on the other hand, was not. He pulled his phone out of the pocket of his black slacks. "I'm calling it in. You… people are going to jail. All of you. We'll transport you to county lockup if we have to."

"Thorn, no," I said, but he was retreating to the car.

Probably to get his service weapon. I could protect our girls, but I understood why he wouldn't take the chance. And I couldn't ask him to…

"Put them in a jar!" Amelda screamed.

I took a deep breath. "You should leave now," I said in low warning, in hopes that they would get scared and leave. "Everything you believe about us is true, and things are about to get very bad for you."

Too bad they were too stupid to be scared. "The Lord will protect us!"

I hated to tell these idiots, but no higher power was going to protect their hateful…behinds. What they were doing was not Christianity. It was far from it.

And right on cue, a spell chant started to rise up behind me. "No, you guys. Stop it!" I pleaded with the witches.

But it was no use. I couldn't be mad at them, but I really did want them to stop. I wouldn't join them, but I wouldn't lift my voice to help either.

I turned around to see Thorn marching back to the protest line with his phone up to his ear. His weapon was in his hand but at his side.

"I'm going to need…" he said into the phone, but then stopped.

Because before he could get the rest of it out, the dozens of protestors lined up at the cemetery gates poofed. And in their place was a herd of bleating goats.

"You guys!" I said and turned to address my family and coven. "You really shouldn't have done that."

"Sacrifice them to Satan!" one of the more Lilith-like members of the family howled, and then followed up with a cackle.

So, the goats were goats, but they were also still the protesters. Sentient, conscious goats that understood everything we were saying. And when someone threatened to sacrifice them, they took off in every direction.

"Stop them!" I called out. "Come on, you guys. I know you're hurting, but we need to contain this."

"Never mind," Thorn said into the phone. "It was a false alarm. Don't send anyone," he added before hanging up with dispatch.

"Mom, you can't turn them back. They'll tell everybody," Laney said as she tugged at my hand. She had Bonkers tucked under her other arm like a football.

"Yeah, and they deserve it," Hekate added. "Let them be goats. At least they can't do any more stupid protests."

"You guys, we cannot leave them as goats. We've got to round them up and turn them back. We'll have to do a memory wipe, but it won't take much. The veil over town will help us make them forget."

"That's a huge undertaking," Amelda said as she joined my little family circle. "We'll have to plan something like that out, and then make sure we have the energy and resources for it. Everyone is wiped out now. We need food, and rest, and time to mourn."

She was right. We needed to head back to Lilith's house for the after-funeral party. There would be plenty of food and people could rest.

Figuring out the goat thing would wait a little while. I was sure having a herd of sentient goats wandering around Coventry wouldn't be the strangest event the town had ever seen.

That award went to Bonkers. He'd wiggled free of Laney's clutches and was twenty feet outside of the cemetery riding one of the goats.

The goat was not happy.

Chapter Five

Since the goats had scattered, everyone was able to
leave the cemetery. A few people stopped to clean up
the signs they'd dropped, and after we got to Lilith's
house, they started a bonfire in the backyard. It was
cathartic for them to burn the signs. I figured it was
healthy.

The energy at Lilith's house was a little lighter than at
the funeral. People joked about her shenanigans. The
mood lightened because everyone realized Lilith
wouldn't want them sitting around crying.

Plus, she had a huge, fully stocked liquor cabinet. The
drinks began to flow. Someone showed up with a
cake. Someone else turned on music.

At first, I wasn't sure about it, but I too quickly
realized they were throwing the kind of party that
would make Lilith proud. I thought the neighbors
might call the police, but as the party raged on, they
all sort of trickled in and joined the merriment.

I was walking past the front door to go upstairs and
check on the girls, all of the kids who stayed had been
sent upstairs for their own no-alcohol party, when I
heard a knock at the door. I thought it was strange.
No one had been knocking. At some point, it was

obvious that the party was open invite, and people just let themselves in.

But there it was again. For sure, someone was knocking at the front door. "Come in!" I called, but that was followed with another staccato round of knocks.

I worried a little that perhaps whoever, or whatever, was out there couldn't come in. A little chill ran down my spine.

Whatever it was, it had to be dealt with because they knocked again. So, I straightened the wrinkles out of my dress and pushed a lock of my hair off my forehead before opening the door.

At first, it didn't register. I thought that perhaps I was just looking at a reflection of myself in the glass storm door, but then I remembered that Lilith didn't have a storm door.

And while the woman standing on the porch looked a lot like me, she wasn't an exact twin. We did have the same wavy red hair, but her nose was a little more pinched. Her lips were a touch fuller. And her eyes burned bright lavender.

A gasp escaped my lips when I realized who she looked like. It was like looking back in time at a Lilith that was eighty years younger.

She was ethereal and timeless. Younger, but by how much? The woman before me could have been a touch over eighteen from one angle and thirty from another.

But who was she? Because I recognized her, but at the same time, I'd never seen the woman in Coventry before.

"Can I help you?" I asked and stepped back so the woman could enter. It was obvious she was family. Maybe from out of town? A distant relative I'd never heard of that looked like she could be Lilith's and my twin…

"I guess I'm here for the party," she snarked, and I recognized her voice instantly. It was Lilith's.

But how?

"Lilith?" I asked tentatively.

"Oh, so you do know me. Okay, then. I have to wonder why, if you know who I am, are you all having a party inside of my house without me?" she said as she stepped over the threshold.

The house went completely silent. All eyes turned toward the front door. We remained there, suspended in quiet, for what felt like an hour.

"Lilith!" someone called from the top of the stairs and broke the absolute stillness.

I turned and realized it was Hekate. She smiled and then practically threw herself down the stairs.

When she reached the bottom, Lilith opened her arms and folded my daughter into a tight embrace.

After a few beats of hesitation, I joined them. I didn't know what was going on, but the relief of seeing Lilith again, even if it was in a new form, was palpable.

"You're back," I said. "But how?"

"I don't know," Lilith said as she released me and Hekate, but I noticed that she gave Hekate a wink.

Did she know more than she let on? Or was that just a special communication between herself and one of her favorite children?

"You were murdered," I said softly. "Do you know who did it? We can take care of right away."

"I don't," she said. "I don't remember anything about... well, anything after I sent you to the store to get the jimsonweed."

"You were doing some sort of ritual," I said trying to jog her memory. "You needed supplies, so you sent me out. When I got back, you were... gone."

"I don't remember," she said. "But speaking of food, I'm famished. I do believe I've never eaten in this body before."

Well, that cleared one thing up. She wasn't the same body we'd just put in the ground, but it opened up a ton more questions. One being, where had she gotten a brand-new body? A body that looked exactly like the old Lilith but younger. Had she done this before? But those were questions that could wait until she'd had something to eat.

"Oh, of course. We have lots of food here. We actually just had your funeral," I said.

"I was wondering what all of the fuss was about. Why all of you were in my house having a party," she waved at all of the coven who were still standing around staring with their mouths agape.

Amelda pushed her way through the crowd and looked Lilith over. Eventually, she must have been satisfied that her sister was the real deal. "Come on! Let's get you something to eat. And maybe a drink."

"Do you have tacos?" Lilith asked.

"Oh… uh, no," Amelda answered. "We have fried chicken, potatoes of many varieties, and cold salads. Oh, and someone brought a cake."

"I'll take a rum and Coke… and some tacos. I'm just dying for the ones from the Mexican restaurant," Lilith chuckled. "I guess that's a poor choice of words."

"You can't go out," Amelda said. "Not until we talk this all over. We have to have a coven meeting first. You understand."

"I want tacos," Lilith stated plainly. "I came back from the dead, and somebody better have some tacos."

"I'll go," I volunteered. "I'll go to the Mexican place and get tacos."

"I'll go with you," Thorn volunteered.

"No, you stay with the girls. I'll be okay," I said. "I'll get the tacos and I'll come right back."

"You sure?" he asked.

"I'll take Meri," I said.

Meri came running through the crowd. "Shotgun!" he called unnecessarily because we were the only ones going.

"You got it," I answered instead of correcting him. "I'll get the tacos and be right back," I reassured Thorn. "I need some air."

Thorn kissed me, and Meri and I took off. We got into the car and carefully backed around the few dozen vehicles lining Lilith's street. There were nowhere close to as many people at the house as there were at the funeral, but there was still a mass of people.

I was relieved to get out for a few minutes and get some space from the situation. "I miss my friends," I said to Meri as we drove down the street.

I'd wanted Viv, Reggie, and Dorian to attend the funeral, but the whole affair was witches only. It was the custom when someone of Lilith's status died. I thought about breaking it, but many of the elders had expressed their discomfort with the idea.

So, I sucked it up and made it through the day without them. We were all planning to meet up at Hangman's House for dinner and a cookout. I wasn't quite sure how that would go with Lilith being back.

"You're doing great," Meri said, and his uncharacteristic kindness made me side-eye him.

"What? I think this is all weird too. I'd say you're handling it like a champ."

"First of all, you're being too nice. It scares me when you're this unsarcastic. Second, I practically ran out of the house to get tacos."

"When a woman comes back from the dead and wants tacos, you get her tacos," Meri said.

At that point, I pulled into the parking lot at the Mexican place and turned the car off. "Do you think it's really her?" I asked without getting out of the car.

"I mean, who else would it be?" Meri asked.

"Someone or something pretending to be her," I posited.

"How would they get in?" Meri asked. "Her house is extremely warded. And even if they did, why? Free tacos?"

"I'd do a lot for free tacos, but probably not impersonating a dead person," I answered. "And maybe that's why she knocked? I thought that part was strange."

"Yeah, but the way Hekate ran to her. That girl knew. She has a sense about things."

"That's true," I agreed.

"Besides, if it's not really Lilith, then she's going to be in a whole heap of hurting. Just walking into a house full of powerful witches like that. They'll figure it out and turn her into mincemeat before we get back."

"Maybe we should get back, then," I said and opened the car door. "I'll make it quick."

"Don't forget my nachos," Meri said.

"Your nachos?"

"Yeah, with extra beef and black beans."

"Have you been replaced by a pod cat?"

"What? I like to branch out every once in a while. I like nachos."

"Bonkers is working you away from your all-meat diet," I said with a chuckle. "He's getting you hooked on carbs."

"That crazy cat has nothing to do with it," Meri sniped.

"Whatever," I said and closed the door.

"Whatever," Meri retorted, but the door shutting mostly muffled it.

I walked inside the restaurant and my stomach growled. I hadn't really eaten much that day. While that was unusual for me, I'd been under a lot of stress. Even after the funeral, I'd just barely picked at a bowl of cheesy potatoes.

When I stepped up to the counter, I ordered Meri's nachos first, and then two party packs of the tacos. It wouldn't be enough for everyone, but a few of the kids hadn't wanted what we were serving at the funeral lunch. I figured I could take some of the Mexican food up to them.

Plus, I'd eat a few tacos myself. That's one thing I definitely agreed with Lilith on. The tacos from this joint were superb. The red sauce they slathered on them took the simple food up to another level.

I sat at a table and waited for them prepare what turned out to be a huge order. One of the employees brought me out a cup and said I could have a drink on the house while I waited. I got up and filled it with ice and Coke before returning to my little table to wait.

While I sat there poking the straw in and out of the lid, a couple came and sat down at the table next to me. They immediately started talking about Lilith.

That was when I realized that I'd either been looking out the window or down at my cup. They had no idea who sat at the table next to them.

"I heard she bought it because she stole a bunch of money," the woman said with a little too much excitement.

Small-town gossip was practically a sport, so I tried not to let it bother me. I kept my emotions in check and listened in because I still needed to figure out who killed Lilith. She might be back, but that didn't mean the killer wouldn't try again.

"That's ridiculous," the man answered. "That whole family is loaded. They own everything in this town already."

We didn't.

"I also heard that she stole Cassandra Minton's husband," the woman said with a chuckle.

"You've got to be kidding. That woman was like a thousand years old. She hasn't stolen anyone's husband for a few decades."

Rude.

"Yeah, well, for some reason, Wayde Barlow was telling people he was glad she was gone."

"Wayde Barlow? The farmer? Why would he have been happy she was gone?"

"Word is that she was blackmailing him into letting her grow drugs on his land. Just a little patch of a field surrounded by his other crops. She made him let her do it, and he hated her for it."

"Drugs?" the man asked skeptically. "That sounds farfetched."

"Maybe not just drugs. Like poisonous plants too. I heard the plants killed one of his prize heifers. That Lilith woman paid him for the cow, but it made their bad blood worse. Wayde begged her to stop using his field, but she wouldn't let it go."

"That sounds like a fairy story," the man said.

But I wasn't so sure. This woman was giving an awful lot of detail for a made-up story. It was enough to make me think it just might be real.

"But Aileen Wolf saw the field one time. She said it was full of drugs and weird plants."

"Aileen, that strange receptionist at the orthopedic clinic?"

"Yeah. When I'd go in there to get my ankle checked, we'd get to talking," the woman said.

But before they could go on, a guy from the restaurant brought me my three large bags of food. He set them down on the table with flourish, and the couple turned and looked at me. The man went pale, and his wife's cheeks burned red.

"I'm sorry," the man stammered, but his wife just swallowed hard.

"Have a good day," I said and picked up my bags.

I made my way out to the car and put the bags on the floor in the back seat.

"Did you buy everything?" Meri snarked as I adjusted them.

"I'm hungry, and some of the kids wanted something other than fried chicken," I said.

"Did you get my nachos?"

"Of course," I said, but I hadn't checked the bags.

I did that really quick and found that they'd gotten the entire order correct. I rolled the tops of the brown paper bags back down and stood up to shut the car door.

"Hey, give me my nachos," Meri protested.

"Not in the car," I said and shut the door. "You can wait until we get back to Lilith's," I continued as I slid behind the steering wheel.

"You're the worst," Meri protested.

"That's better. I was wondering how long you could hold out being nice."

"I did my best," he replied.

On the way back to Lilith's house, I told him what I'd overheard in the Mexican restaurant. We were pulling into the driveway when I finally finished the story. It was a good thing my husband, the sheriff, was in the house because I'd probably sped a little too much.

"So, Lilith has a field of poison plants and drugs? That's not exactly shocking. You've met her, right?"

"It just feels like I should do something with that information," I said.

"What you should do is go in the house and get me my nachos."

"Fine," I said.

I got out of the car and grabbed the food from the back seat. When I stood up, I heard a sound from behind me.

It took a few seconds for me to realize it was the sound of hooves on the grass and concrete driveway. When I turned around, six goats stood in a semi-circle staring at me.

"Oh, no," I said and started backing up.

One of them bleated, and they all started scraping their front hooves across the ground. They appeared to be about ready to charge.

What an absolute pain in the butt. I'd have to use magic to stop them without hurting them. But I was so drained already.

Meri jumped in front of me. "Run for the house," he said to me and then turned to hiss at the goats.

"You don't have to tell me twice," I said and pivoted.

The goats started to charge anyway, but I kept running. The sounds of a scuffle erupted behind me.

When I got to the front door, I realized my hands were full. I had to set a bag down and open the door.

As I did, Meri came running from behind and leapt over the bag. "All done," he said smugly as he skidded to a stop in the house.

I turned to look, and sure enough, the goats were all running away down the street. Thorn appeared from the living room. He took the bags from my hands and I picked up the one off the porch.

Lilith waited in the kitchen eager for her tacos. I took six out of the bag and laid them out on the table for her. I'd expected her to be surrounded by family, but it was just her, Amelda, and my mom and dad in the kitchen.

"I got extra," I said. "Some of the kids upstairs didn't want the fried chicken."

"I'll take it up to them," Dad volunteered.

"There's a cheese quesadilla in there for Bonkers too," I said and noticed that everyone looked a little strained.

Mom and Amelda were shooting each other dirty looks. Lilith looked pleased.

"I'll make sure he gets it," Dad said, and he hurried out of the room.

Thankfully, I'd set a few tacos aside for myself. But I had to get to the bottom of what was going on in that kitchen before I dug in.

"What's going on?" I asked. "You could cut the tension in the air with a knife."

"Amelda, and some of the other Aunties, think that we should just move on since I'm here and alive and eating tacos," Lilith said before she took a huge bite.

"And I think that's ridiculous," Mom practically growled. "There's a killer on the loose. We don't just need justice. We need vengeance. They killed Lilith!"

"Well, technically, Lilith isn't really dead," Amelda said in a cool, authoritative tone. "She's right here."

"But someone managed to get into her house and kill her," I argued. "And when they find out they didn't really do the job, who's to say they won't be back?"

"How do you know that Lilith wasn't just the first victim?" Mom yelled. "Have you all lost your minds?"

Dad appeared in the kitchen. He put her arm around mom. "Please calm down, Brighton. You're scaring the children."

I thought she was going to shrug him off, but instead, she sort of slumped into him. Dad kissed her on her temple, and Mom visibly relaxed a little more.

"What's going to scare them more is if a killer comes after their parents. Or even worse, if they come after the children. How do you know that's not going to happen?"

"Let's not get ahead of ourselves, dear," Amelda said, and I saw my mother stiffen again.

"Yeah, I mean, I had a lot of enemies," Lilith said with a mouth full of taco. "Well, I don't know if they were enemies, but I made a lot of people mad just in my daily life. I'd guess it was personal and not some witch serial killer."

"Well, then who?" Mom demanded. "Who did this to you?"

"I really don't know," Lilith said and went back to eating her taco.

"Can I say something?" Thorn asked and every head in the kitchen swiveled around to glare at him. He held up his hands in mock surrender. "Sorry, I just have something to contribute. Something that might change the discussion."

"What is it?" Mom demanded.

"My department won't be investigating Lilith's death."

"What?" I turned around to fully face him and put my hands on my hips. "I mean, that's fine, but why?

Because she's here now? How are you going to explain that away? We have to come up with something…"

Thorn cut me off. "It's not because she's here now, sweetie. It's because the medical examiner ruled her death a suicide."

"You're all insane," Mom said and stormed out of the kitchen.

And then out of the house.

Chapter Six

Brighton

They'd all lost their ever-loving minds. And I felt like I'd begun to lose my grip too.

There was the new, younger Lilith sitting at her kitchen table munching on tacos like she hadn't just come back from the dead. If I hadn't been so happy to see her, I would have slapped her.

But it was so confusing. And nobody was talking about how or why it happened.

Probably because it wasn't the most pressing matter. That had to be who killed her.

I refused to go along with the Aunties' suggestion to just let it go. While the notion that we had a witch serial killer in our midst was kinda far out, it wasn't impossible. It wasn't worth the risk.

The rage I kept feeling towards everyone in the situation kept bubbling up in my chest, and I truly did not want to scare the children, so I left. Remy would have to get a ride because I hopped in the car and peeled out of there.

I wasn't going to sit around and wait for the Aunties to convince Kinsley to let Lilith's murder go. And it was a murder. I don't care what my son-in-law sheriff said. There was no way Lilith killed herself.

She was into some dark things, but she didn't want to die. Heck, that was one of the reasons the old goat still hung on. And after we'd almost lost her to that dementia incident, she'd taken good care of herself in a way only a witch can.

Suicidal people didn't do that. And even if she was considering that, she'd have told someone. She'd have talked to me or Kinsley. She wouldn't just… do that.

So, I drove. I drove my car around town for a few minutes, and then pulled over to the curb and turned off the engine.

When I took a good look around, I realized I was parked down the block from the house of one Charity Lubbox. The story of her accosting my daughter had made it back to me.

If she hated Lilith enough to go after Kinsley in a grocery store parking lot, then she was someone I needed to speak with. Or perhaps she was just that desperate for money.

Desperate enough to kill?

No one could have broken into Lilith's house to poison her, but if she had a client come knocking at her door, then she would have welcomed the woman in. If Charity had spun a story about repeat business, then Lilith would have taken it.

I was getting out of the driver's side of the car when a black streak whooshed out the back seat and past me. Meri sat near my feet on the sidewalk flicking his tail.

"You had to get out of there too, huh?" I asked.

"Just keeping an eye on you. I heard the argument in the kitchen, and when you stormed out, I decided to follow."

"I didn't storm out," I protested.

"Oh, yes, you did. You flounced out of there with drama."

"I did not."

"Did too," Meri licked his paw and casually cleaned his ear.

"Whatever," I said and brushed past him.

"Whatever," he mocked me with a bad impersonation.

I ignored him and kept walking. We were there on very important investigative and coven business, and I wasn't about to waste a bunch of time arguing on the sidewalk with the cat.

Charity's house was like a lot of older houses in Coventry. It was a two-story Victorian, but smaller than Lilith's house. It could have used a coat of paint and someone to pull the weeds, but other than that, the turquoise house with ornate black trim was pretty.

Meri and I made our way up the front steps, and I rang the bell. When no one answered, I rang it again. I was about to give up when the door finally cracked open a couple of inches.

"What do you want?" Charity asked as she peered out the door with one eye.

"I came to talk to you," I answered. "Can I come in?"

"No," she said and slammed the door.

I stood there for a moment wondering what to do. I was about to knock again when the door opened a crack.

"What do you want?" Charity asked again as if the previous encounter had never happened.

I took a deep breath and tried not to sound annoyed. I wanted information, so I needed this woman on my side. Or at the very least, I needed her to believe I was on hers.

"I'm concerned about what my Aunt Lilith did to you," I lied. "And I was hoping we could have a talk and make things right. My daughter told me what happened earlier, and I don't agree with the way she treated you. That girl can be a handful." I felt bad throwing Kinsley under the bus like that, but sometimes a witch had to do what she had to do.

"Would you like some iced tea?" Charity said as she swung the door open enthusiastically.

That was too easy...

I stepped into her cluttered foyer as Charity turned and walked down a hallway. I nearly tripped over a pair of shoes that were only partially against the wall, but I managed not to fall and followed her. The breeze created by us both walking quickly knocked a stack of mail off her entry table.

Charity cast a look back over her shoulder but kept going. Part of me wanted to pick it up, but it wasn't my house. A few seconds later, we made an abrupt left and found ourselves in a kitchen that was thankfully cleaner than the foyer. Not by much, but at least it wasn't filthy.

She busied herself grabbing a couple of glasses from a cabinet and then filling them from a pitcher of iced tea from the fridge. I leaned against a counter and fought the urge to straighten boxes of food and bottles scattered on the surfaces around me.

Charity handed me a glass. "It's already sweet. I hope that's okay."

"It's fine, thank you," I said and set the glass down on the counter in a clear spot.

"I'd invite you to sit down, but…" she trailed off.

She didn't need to elaborate. The kitchen table was covered in boxes, three piles of mail, and a stack of multi-colored mixing bowls. They were clean, but just not put away.

"It's fine. It's good to stand," I said and reached for the iced tea before thinking better of it. "I heard you were looking for a refund for a potion Lilith made for you?"

Sometimes, the best approach was the direct approach. I suddenly found myself wanting to get out of there. Despite the kitchen seeming cleaner than the foyer, a strange, sour smell had wound its way to my nose.

"Yeah, and your daughter blew me off," she said and took a gulp of her tea. At least I knew it wasn't poisoned because I'd watched her pour the glasses herself.

"I heard about that, and I'm sorry. I just wanted to know if there was something I could do to make amends."

"You can give me a refund. Same thing I asked your girl for," Charity said before taking another glug of her tea. That one left her glass more than half empty.

"Well, I don't have a thousand dollars on me, but we can talk… By any chance, did you visit Lilith recently and ask for a refund?" I asked as nonchalantly as I could.

Charity's eyes narrowed and she practically slammed her glass of tea down on the table between the biggest pile of mail and the mixing bowls. The action sent the better part of the pile to the floor, where Charity kicked it under the table, before turning her attention back to me.

"I did, but what are you getting at?"

"I'm not getting at anything," I said. "I'm just trying to figure out what happened to Lilith, and I wondered if maybe you knew something. Maybe you saw something or she said…"

"No, you're not!" Charity said and took a step toward me.

"I'm not what?" I asked and hoped I didn't have to use magic on this clearly unhinged woman. But I totally would if she pushed me.

"You're not curious if I know something or if I saw something. You're accusing me of doing it. You're trying to frame me!"

"I am not," I said and took a sidestep toward the hallway. "I really do want to make things right, but I was hoping we could help each other."

"NO! You're just like them. You don't think that witch did anything wrong. You think my Joe left me because I'm a bad housekeeper and I can get a little emotional! You don't believe me that she drove him away!"

"Why? Why would Lilith do that?" I had to know why this woman thought Lilith would even care about her marriage.

"I... I don't know..." Charity faltered. Was it possible she was about to have a breakthrough?

"See?"

"No! Stop. You're trying to confuse me," Charity said with a shake of her head.

"I'm not," I said earnestly. "I just really want to know what happened to my aunt, and if you can help me..."

"Get out!" Charity roared. "Get out of my house now!"

So I did. But I didn't leave.

It was a nice day, so Charity had a few of her windows open. I know what you're thinking, and no, I didn't try to break back in.

But I could hear her pacing around the house, cursing and knocking things over. She was properly in a rage.

So, I skulked around the outside of her house. I wasn't sure why, but something told me not to leave until I checked out her yard and garage.

Her car was parked in the driveway, and I nearly missed something as I hurried past it. But as I reached for the garage door, I got a picture in my mind.

Something in the back seat of Charity's car. So I hurried back over to get a good look.

And sure enough, my brain hadn't failed me. Sitting right on her backseat, on the driver's side, was Lilith's garden gnome.

How did I know it was Lilith's? Well, because she was the only person I knew with a garden gnome dressed as Michael Myers. You know, from the Halloween movies?

For some reason, Charity had stolen it.

I was going to go back and knock on her front door, but I didn't have to. As soon as I grabbed the gnome from the car and slammed the door shut, Charity was rounding the corner onto the driveway.

"What are you doing?" she wailed loud enough for the entire neighborhood to hear.

"You stole this from Lilith's yard," I accused. "So what else did you do to her?"

"I…" Charity sputtered, "I didn't steal it. I ordered it off the internet!"

"Oh, yeah?"

"Yeah."

"Then why is it in your car?"

She thought about it for a moment. "Because the delivery driver didn't leave it. I had to go to the FedEx place over in Decatur to pick it up."

"So, you opened the box, took it out, and left it in your car? Where's the box? Why would you take the box out of your car and leave this in it?" I asked as I thrust the garden gnome toward her. "That makes no sense."

"She owed me!" was Charity's reply. "I wanted it, so I took it. Because she owed me."

"Well, now I've caught you lying and stealing. So what else could you have done?"

"None of that proves anything," Charity hissed. "And if you're trying to imply that I killed her, why would I do that? All I want is my money back. She can't give it to me now, and the rest of your family is useless."

I wanted to say something back to that, but she was kind of right. If she wanted money, then killing Lilith wasn't the best way to kill her.

She could have flown into a rage, but who rage killed someone with poison in their Diet Coke? That theory didn't really hold water either.

"I'm going to go," I said in defeat. "But I'm taking this with me, and if I find out any information that indicates you did this, I'll be back."

"Good riddance," Charity said as I brushed past her.

Chapter Seven

Brighton

When I got back to Lilith's house, I was able to park in the driveway. It seemed that quite a few people had left. I wondered how many of them had just shown up for the free food and then felt relieved of any guilt about taking off now that Lilith was officially alive.

I put the gnome in her front landscaping before going into the house. Meri gave it a sniff before trailing me through the front door.

Things inside the house still felt tense. There were a few stragglers hanging out in the living room, and I could hear some of the kids playing upstairs.

Everyone I'd left in the kitchen was still there, but there was a new edition. Aqua Skeenbauer stood in the middle of the room giving everyone dirty looks. They were returned in kind, and my family looked like predators surrounding prey.

Ready to pounce.

Apparently, I'd missed something and had returned during a lull in the drama. No one spoke, though. It was as if the pause button had been pushed on an argument.

"What's going on here?" seemed like the most reasonable question to ask. "We're all family here.

Why do you guys look like you want to rip each other apart?"

"Have a good time?" Lilith asked with a snarky smile.

"Well, I found out that your old friend Charity Lubbox is a lying thief, but she probably didn't kill you," I said. "What I meant was, what's going on here? You could cut the tension like a cake."

"Charity, oh," Lilith let out a cackle. "She's nuts. I mean, her grip has really slipped, but she thought it was my fault her husband left her. Hah! She said she wanted him to stop cheating on her, and I'd say that he's not anymore. Mission successful."

"So, you can remember that, but nothing about who might have poisoned you?" Amelda pressed.

"I thought you didn't care," I shot at her. "I thought you said we should all just let this go."

"Well, apparently, that's not going to happen. So, if Lilith could just tell us who did this, we could take care of the problem, and move on with our lives."

"I already told you, sister, I don't remember."

"See, this is the problem," Aqua roared. "All of this fuss for… for her!"

"What's your problem with Lilith?" I asked.

"I've already been over this!" she yelled.

103

"Well, apparently, I missed it. So, somebody fill me in," I replied.

"Laney and Thorn heard Aqua cursing at Lilith's body at the funeral," Kinsley said gently. "And I noticed she was acting strange too."

"I wasn't acting strange," Aqua corrected. "I was acting like I didn't care that she was dead. Which I didn't. Can't say I'm too glad she's back either."

"Whoa, okay. Let's back this train up a little bit," I said and stepped between Aqua and Lilith. I wasn't a hundred percent sure, but it seemed like something was about to go down. "Aqua, I didn't know you were having problems with Lilith. This is the first I've heard of it, so why don't you fill me in."

"I don't want to talk about this anymore! I just want to leave!" Aqua shrieked loud enough that the noises of the kids playing upstairs came to a halt.

"I'm going to go check on them," Thorn said.

"Why don't you take them outside?" Kinsley suggested.

"That's a good idea," he replied and exited the room.

"Mom," Kinsley began, "apparently, old Lilith taught Aqua's son a summoning spell."

"And?" I asked. "We're witches. We all know a few summoning spells."

"She taught him to summon a tuba-playing ghost," Aqua yelled. "And that's not all. She went on a date with Laramie."

"It wasn't a date," Lilith said.

"He took you out to dinner and paid for it," Aqua said. "That's a date. And I can't prove it, but I know you guys went to the Motel 6 after."

"Laramie? As in your boyfriend?" I asked Aqua.

"Ex now. She ruined everything."

Lilith just shrugged.

"Really?! That's all I get is a shrug? After you ruined the best chance I had at marriage in years!" Aqua was livid.

She lunged at Lilith, but Kinsley stood her ground. Everybody needed to calm down before it came to blows.

"And I seriously doubt that Lilith went to a Motel 6," Kinsley added. "That just sounds farfetched. We don't even have one in Coventry."

All eyes fell on Lilith. "That's why we chose that motel. It's in another town, so I figured no one would see us. Turns out it's a regular hot spot for people from Coventry who don't want anyone to know who that are... spending time with. Plus, Laramie paid, and he's not exactly made of money."

Aqua lunged at Lilith again, but Kinsley held her back. "Stop," she said and put her hand on Aqua's chest. "I know you're upset but you need to stop. I'm going to have to deal with you if you try to get at her one more time."

That seemed to knock some of the wind out of Aqua's sails. "I can't believe that type of behavior is condoned in this family."

"I did you a favor," Lilith said. "He was cheap and untrustworthy. Can you imagine if you had married him?"

Aqua didn't make a move at Lilith again, but I could swear steam came out of her ears. "You bewitched him!"

"Oh, please," Lilith said, and this time she stood up from her chair. "Don't use that medieval crap with me. Do you know how many of our sister ancestors burned because of accusations like that?" Lilith's eyes darkened, and for just a moment, you could really see why some people thought she was the actual queen of demons. "I had some fun. Probably not as much as if I'd chosen a better companion, but the fact of the matter remains that he and I were both consenting adults. And… I did you a favor. He would have broken your heart."

"Lilith, that's still pretty trashy," Kinsley said.

"Well, that was the old me," Lilith said and smacked her lips. "I'll try to do better this time around."

Kinsley

"Aqua, she's right, though," I finally reluctantly admitted. "He would have broken your heart. I know it hurts, but that man was no good for you."

"She didn't have to make me find out that way," Aqua said and crossed her arms over her chest.

"What other way would you have listened?" Lilith asked. "People tried to tell you. I tried to tell you."

"This is not productive," Mom said.

"I'm outta here," Aqua said with a huff, and thankfully, she left.

I felt bad for her, I really did, but her drama was giving me a headache. I'd had enough for the day.

"Mom, where were you?" I asked once Aqua was gone for sure.

"I went to go see Charity Lubbox," Mom said. "I thought I already mentioned that."

"Right, sorry," I said and pinched the bridge of my nose.

"Sit down, sweetie. Let me get you something to drink. Did you ever eat?"

"I didn't," I admitted. "My food is still in the bag."

"I'll get it. Just sit."

I watched as Mom whirled around the kitchen fixing me a plate of food. My instinct was to get up and help her, but I fought it. Instead, I rubbed my temples and tried to relax the tension in my shoulders.

When Mom finally set the plate down in front of me, I dug in. I hadn't realized how hungry I was until I started eating.

A few minutes in, and the food was gone. It was about the time Lilith reappeared in the kitchen doorway, she'd excused herself to her powder room, and announced that she needed some rest.

That was our cue to go home. Everyone seemed reluctant to leave her alone, but what could we do? As much as a few of us wanted to babysit her until we found the killer, Lilith would never allow it.

So, eventually, we said our goodbyes and made our way out to the cars. Mom stood by her car staring at the house for a good while until Dad talked her into getting in.

We drove about halfway home before Bonkers jumped up on the front dash and shrieked, "Stop the car!"

"Bonkers, what's wrong?" Laney asked as she started to unbuckle her seatbelt.

"No, Laney, stay buckled in," I said and reached for Bonkers.

He evaded me and ran over in front of the steering wheel. Thorn had no choice but to pull the car over.

"There's an ambush!" Bonkers yelled.

I looked ahead at the street that led to ours and saw nothing. We were all used to Bonkers' occasional outbursts, but at times, they were wildly inconvenient.

"Bonkers, get back in the back with the girls," Thorn said and reached for him.

But the fat orange cat only scrambled over to the side of the dash in front of me. Around that time, Meri perked up and sniffed the air.

"No, he's right," Meri said and stood up on my lap. He'd been curled up on my legs for the ride home since Hekate was looking at a book she'd borrowed from Lilith's library.

"What are you two talking about?" I demanded. "An ambush? On Vine Street? There's nothing around. You two need to cut it out right now. This isn't the time for your shenanigans."

"Cut it out right meow!" Bonkers mocked me and then turned back to watch out the front windshield.

Before I could scold him, something rustled in the bushes on the side of the road about fifty feet in front of us. At first, I'd thought I'd imagined it. There was a whole line of shrubbery and flowering plants lining the side of the road, and it all began to swish.

And then they appeared. About a half-dozen goats stepped out of the bushes and lined up in the middle of the road. Another fifty feet ahead, about ten more emerged from those bushes and moved to flank us.

"Goats," Thorn grumbled. "Freaking goats."

Suddenly, Hekate unbuckled from her booster seat and jumped out of the car. Her book flew off to the side and landed in the seat between her seat and her sister.

She ran toward the goats. I tried to leap out of the car to follow her, but I forgot to unbuckle my own seatbelt. It took me a good few seconds to realize why I was stuck in my seat because my first thoughts were that the goats had somehow obtained magic powers and pinned me in the car.

"Your seatbelt," Thorn said gently as he opened his car door.

He got out first, but I was soon to follow.

"What should I do?" Laney cried out before I could close my door.

That gave Meri time to slip out and run to Thorn and Hekate. Bonkers sensed Laney's distress and leapt off the dashboard. He crossed the console and jumped into her lap.

"Stay in the car with Bonkers," I said, and she sniffled. "They're just goats but stay here with Bonkers."

I could tell she was mulling it over as I slammed my door shut. On the one hand, she'd never live it down with her little sister that she'd stayed in the car and done nothing. On the other, I told her to stay put. Laney listened and followed the rules, so that's what she did.

The goats had closed ranks and were either stomping their feet or scratching their front hooves on the road. Just like the ones earlier when they were about to charge.

I hadn't noticed, but Thorn had grabbed his service weapon from the glove box. "Thorn, you're not going to shoot them," I said. "They're goats."

"They're not just goats," he answered. "They're in some sort of attack formation."

"They're still just goats. Well, actually, they're people too, remember?"

"Awful people," Hekate said completely deadpan.

"Sweetie, that still doesn't mean we can shoot them."

"I will if they charge us," Thorn said more to the goats than to us.

"I got this," Hekate said with a shrug.

She raised her hands and extended her fingers. I tried to listen as she whispered something... some dark incantation... under her breath. But the more I tried to hone in on her words, the more jumbled they got in my brain.

"Hekate, what are you doing?" Thorn's voice was edged with concern, and to me, it sounded almost like he was underwater.

I understood that it was the sound of his voice trying to travel through the pulsating magic surrounding Hekate. It was like a purple mist, and if you looked at it just right, you could almost see tiny lightning bolts flashing through the miasma.

"Don't kill them," I pleaded and suddenly found myself almost afraid.

Of Hekate...

There was so much potential power in her. And she was becoming more and more like Lilith.

But I had to reason that Lilith wasn't dangerous. Not to us, anyway. And neither was Hekate, but I feared for those stupid goats.

I began to draw the magic from inside of me to protect them from Hekate's dark spell, but it was too late. With a growl, she surged forward a few feet and unleased her magic on the goats.

I held my breath and waited for them to fall over. But they didn't. Instead, they shrank to about half of their previous size. Realizing what had just happened to them, the goats bleated, in a much higher pitch, and ran off.

"Mini goats," Hekate said and turned on her heels to go back to the car. "Much less intimidating."

Thorn let out a relieved chuckled. "Good job, sweetie."

I just stood there collecting my thoughts as Hekate got back in the car and buckled in. She picked up her book and started reading again as Thorn took my hand.

"I was a bit worried she might kill them," he whispered to me as we walked back to the car.

"Mini goats," was my reply.

Chapter Eight

Once we got home, the girls went up to their rooms to relax. I headed to the kitchen to start making hamburger patties for Thorn to grill.

I'd gotten exactly two made when Reggie and Jeremy showed up. I'd thought they were going to bring their boys to the cookout, but apparently, they'd gone to stay with Jeremy's family.

So, it was just the two of them. If the girls kept to themselves, which I was reasonably sure they would, then it would be an adult-only party.

"How did it go?" Reggie asked as we stood next to each other at the kitchen counter forming patties.

She'd jumped in and started helping without me even having to ask. Thorn and Jeremy had come in and tried to "help" too, but they only got in the way. We gave them cold beers and chased them outside to get the grill going.

"Anyway, how was the service?" Reggie asked again after they were gone.

"You don't know?"

"Don't know what?" Reggie asked completely seriously.

"How can you not know? Are you messing with me?" I asked.

"Sorry, Kinsley. Are you okay? I haven't heard anything… Jeremy and I drove the kids to visit with his family. I haven't been in town all day. It was the only way he could keep me away from the services."

I loved that Jeremy had to literally take her out of town to keep her away. I could totally see Reggie crashing a funeral full of powerful witches just to be by my side.

"Lilith came back," I finally responded.

"What?" Reggie dropped her hamburger patty, and I barely saved it from falling on the floor. Meri sat at our feet, and I could tell he was bitterly disappointed that I'd rescued the hamburger. "You mean at the funeral? Like she got up? 'Cause I could totally see one of you doing that?"

"One of us?"

"Like someone in your family…" Reggie said. "No offense."

"No, we buried her. But then at the gathering at her house after the services, she showed up. Like, she was knocking on the door."

"That's so weird," Reggie answered. "But I could see it happening."

"But that's not the weirdest part of the story. She's younger. She's like twenty."

"Like she was reborn?" Reggie asked.

"Well, kinda… but like twenty years ago."

"You know some of you witches do like time travel stuff," she reminded me.

"I cannot," I said and sighed. "Not today. I cannot think about Lilith coming back from the dead or time traveling anymore."

"Would you rather talk about the case?" Reggie offered. "Wait, is there even still a case?"

"Not legally. Thorn said the medical examiner ruled it a suicide. Plus, some of the coven want to let it go since she's come back."

"You don't agree," Reggie said. "There's a tone. I'm picking up on a tone."

"I'm not so sure. And Mom is losing her mind over it. My mom has her quirks, but I've never seen her lose it so thoroughly. I mean, I'd love to just let it go and move on with life, but there could also be a witch killer out there. What if we ignore this, and they come back?"

"I can see your point."

"Burgers ready?" Thorn stuck his head in the door and asked.

"Yeah, we're just about done here. Do you guys need another beer?"

"That would be wonderful, beautiful wife," he said and ducked back outside.

"Flattery will get you everywhere," I said even though he was already gone.

Reggie and I put the patties in a pyramid on a plate. We washed our hands and grabbed a couple of beers.

Outside, the guys had the grill ready to go. Even without magic, Thorn could get a pile of coals burning perfectly. He prided himself on it.

"Burger are ready to cook," I said as Reggie set the plate down on the table.

I handed a beer to each of the guys. "Reggie, should we make some margaritas? And maybe some side dishes?"

"We should have taken some of those sides from your mom's house," Thorn said. "There was a ton left over."

"Yeah, probably. Reggie and I can whip something up really quick, though. We've got plenty of ingredients here."

"You had me at margaritas," Reggie said.

We went back inside, and while Reggie mixed some margaritas, I rubbed ears of corn with butter and spices. I ran those outside for Thorn to add to the grill, and when I got back inside, Dorian and Viv had arrived.

"Just in time for margaritas," Dorian said happily.

"Good thing I made extra," Reggie said and handed him the first one.

"Hey, that was supposed to be for me," I protested, but I was only kidding.

"I'm sorry, ma'am, here you go," Dorian said and tried to hand his margarita to me. "The queen of the castle gets the first drink. Where on earth are my manners?"

"It's okay," I said and pushed the drink back toward him. "I just know Reggie is going to make mine next."

"Right after she makes mine!" Viv said with a chuckle.

"Fine," I relented with a smile. "I will be a gracious host and wait for the last margarita."

"You are just too kind," Reggie said and went back to making drinks.

"So…" Dorian said before taking a sip of his cocktail. "I heard a rumor."

"Was that rumor that a woman looking an awful lot like a young Lilith Skeenbauer showed up in town today?" I asked with one eyebrow cocked.

"What?!" Dorian sputtered. "Oh my gawd? Really?"

"That's not what you were going to ask about?"

"We had no idea!" Viv said.

"No, I was going to ask about the rumor that Lilith was blackmailing Wayde Barlow into using his land to grow witchy shi… stuff," Dorian said. "She's alive?"

"She is," I confirmed. "And I've heard that too. I wonder if I need to go talk to him."

"So, you're still on the case?" Viv asked as Reggie handed her a drink.

"Well, of course," Dorian said and playfully elbowed Viv. "There could be a witch killer out there on the loose."

"So, is Lilith coming tonight?" Reggie asked.

"She said she needed to rest," I answered.

"Well, that's probably good," Dorian added. "It would be weird to try to solve her murder with her around."

"Wait, doesn't she know who killed her?" Viv asked.

"She doesn't seem to remember being killed," I said. "At least, that's what she said."

"You don't believe her?" Dorian asked.

"I don't know. I don't think she lying... maybe she's just suppressing it."

"That's understandable," Viv answered before draining half her margarita. "It would be traumatic to remember being killed."

I felt a stab of guilt, and at first I couldn't figure out why. Then it dawned on me. Maybe Lilith's death was traumatic, and by insisting on investigating it, I'd be prolonging her pain.

"You're right," I agreed. "I'll be as gentle as possible, but I still have to figure this out. There's a killer on the loose, and if I don't do anything about it, then I'm not protecting my community."

Just then, the back door opened. "Hey, would any of you like a burger?" Jeremy asked with just his head poked in the kitchen.

"I'll get the girls and be right out."

And then someone started shooting.

The cookout sort of went downhill from there. It wasn't anyone shooting at us.

It turned out to be one of the neighbors trying to gun down a few of the goats. Our neighbors weren't close, but we could hear the shots through the trees that separated our properties.

Thorn and Jeremy got into Thorn's cruiser and headed down to the neighbor's place. The rest of us had to go inside because nobody wanted to catch a stray bullet.

The girls were worried, but I reassured them and sent them to bed. Once they were tucked in, and the shooting stopped, the adults set to making more margaritas.

I was halfway through my second one when there was a knock at the front door. I checked my phone and there was no message from my parents, or anyone else, saying they were dropping by.

"Expecting anyone else?" Dorian asked.

"No," I said and walked to the front door filled with curiosity. "I have no idea who it could be."

"Do you think Thorn left his keys?" Reggie asked.

"He knows where the spare is hidden," I said. "He wouldn't knock."

"Oh, just open the door," Meri groused. "You guys talk way too much."

I rolled my eyes, but he was right. So, I opened the door and found Lilith standing on my front porch. I from earlier hit me like a truck.

"Lilith," I said. "Hello. What are you doing here?"

"I'm here for a visit. Are you going to leave me standing on the front porch like a vacuum salesman?"

"Of course, come in," I said and stepped back so she could enter.

"Oh, margaritas!" Lilith said as soon as she saw the drink in Dorian's hand.

"Would you like one?" Reggie asked. She looked like she'd seen a ghost. As soon as she got the words out of her mouth, it went back to hanging open like a fish gasping for air.

"Could I have strawberry?"

"I..." Reggie basically stammered.

I wasn't sure if it was because of Lilith's appearance or if it was because we all had regular margaritas. It was hard to get a read on her at the moment.

"I have strawberries in the freezer," I jumped in.

"Blended, not shaken," Lilith said with a smile.

She then drifted over to my sofa and made herself comfortable.

Reggie scurried off to the kitchen, and Viv followed close behind her. Dorian and I looked at each other and then sat down on the armchairs flanking the sofa.

"So, Lilith, you look fantastic," Dorian said. "Just remarkable. I mean, you were beautiful before, but wow, I didn't realize that you'd been such a knockout. You are such a knockout."

I threw Dorian a look that I hoped conveyed that he was laying it on a little thick. I didn't know if he caught it or not, but it didn't matter because Lilith ate it up like cheese and crackers.

"Thank you so much," she said and pushed a strand of her glossy fire-engine red hair behind her ear. "It's good to be back."

Had her hair gotten redder? I studied her face and saw that her eyes had deepened to a brilliant amethyst too. In fact, her skin had somehow gotten smoother. It was almost like looking at a living doll. But she didn't seem creepy at all. Just... beautiful.

"Lilith, are you here because you remember something about who killed you?" I asked hopefully.

"Oh, all that?" she asked and waved her hand in front of her face as if trying to dissipate a bad smell. "Aren't you even going to let me get a drink in me before we start with that?"

"Lilith, someone killed you. We need to focus."

"Come to think of it, I'm a bit peckish. Do you have anything to eat?" was her response.

At that point, Meri jumped up on the sofa and sat down next to her. Lilith languidly reached out and stroked his silky black fur.

Traitor. I thought but didn't say.

Then I wondered why I felt that pang of jealousy. Why did I care if Meri got pets from another member of the family? It wasn't like she was going to take him from me.

And that's when I realized why I was so upset. Because I'd been devastated when Lilith died, and shocked when she came back from death, but it almost seemed like she'd re-emerged as a better version of not only herself, but of me…

She looked like me but prettier. I'd run out to get her tacos like I was her personal errand girl and not the head of a powerful coven. My friends were falling all over her. Meri seemed even more content by her side.

What would Thorn think of her? A younger-looking, more beautiful, redheaded witch…

I shook my head. That was stupid.

"Kinsley, dear, did you hear me?" Lilith asked. "Have you got anything to eat?"

"There's always something to eat around here," Dorian said cheerfully.

"I have just about anything you could want," I added a little less cheerfully.

But if Lilith noticed my tone, she didn't let on. "You know what I haven't had in forever?"

"I don't," I responded.

"Chinese food. I could really go for some Mandarin chicken and vegetable lo mein. Oh, and some fried rice and egg rolls."

"I don't have that," I said. "I don't think it's a good time for me to be running out for takeout," I added.

"That's okay," Dorian said. "That new place over near Bella Vita delivers."

"Oh, okay. Well, let me grab my laptop and I'll place an order."

"Don't worry about it. I'll do it," Dorian said and stood up.

"Be a dear and get some of those crab Rangoons too, okay? I love those things," Lilith said.

I waited to see if she was going to offer to pay for her delivery, but Dorian didn't. And she didn't… So, I called after him, "Grab my debit card from my purse. Leave a good tip."

Dorian nodded and then ducked into the dining room to use my laptop. My purse was on the table next to it, so he had everything he needed.

"You don't have to pay," Lilith said, but then she didn't make a move to grab her purse either. It was sitting on the floor next to her feet propped against the sofa, and that's where it stayed.

"It's my treat. You're my guest, and you've been through a lot," I said and tried to sound cheerful.

I didn't know why I was struggling so much to be positive around her. It was just that all of the things that had been endearing about old Lilith were annoying in young Lilith. I couldn't put my finger on why.

"Thank you so much," was her response. By that point, Meri had climbed onto her lap and was snoozing soundly.

Like a traitor.

Reggie and Viv reappeared in the living room. They had a strawberry margarita for Lilith and fresh drinks for themselves. Reggie set the margarita down on the coffee table in front of Lilith, and then the two of them grabbed pillows. They put them down on the floor on the open side of the coffee table and sat.

"So, now that you've got a drink and your food on the way, what did you come here to tell me?" I asked pointedly.

Reggie and Viv took synchronized sips of their margaritas and looked back and forth between me and Lilith. They sensed the tension in me. I could see it in their eyes.

Lilith picked up her margarita and gulped about half of it down. "Wow, that's good. Would probably be better with fresh strawberries, but you did well with what you had."

I bristled.

"You're welcome?" Reggie sounded kinda snarky, and I was proud of her for it.

"Anyway," Lilith said and sat the glass back down on the coffee table. "Someone came to see me after all of you left."

Dorian came back in the room just then and took his seat in the armchair. "I ordered the food. They said it would be about twenty minutes."

"Were you able to get the crab Rangoon?" Lilith asked.

"I sure was. I got double of everything in case someone else wants some too. Since our cookout got interrupted."

"Oh, the cookout. I'm so sorry that didn't go well," Lilith said. "What happened?"

"We don't know for sure," I said. "One of the neighbors was shooting at something."

"Probably those goats you were talking about," Viv offered.

"Goats?" Lilith asked as if she hadn't already heard the story, but I knew she probably had.

"Anyway," I said and cleared my throat. I needed to get the conversation back on track. "You said someone came to see you?"

"Oh, right. My neighbor down the block. Her name's Druella or something like that. She believes that I… or rather old me… killed her dog. She came traipsing down demanding to know what I know."

"Did you kill her dog?" I asked because while I didn't think Lilith would do something like that, I was starting to have my doubts about her.

"Of course not," she said with real offense. "But I did put that yappy little thing in a jar."

"Lilith, you didn't."

She shrugged. "I had to. That thing was a menace. More than just a little annoying. Anyway, the dog is fine. It thinks it's in a doggy paradise. I'm not cruel."

"But it's in that doggy paradise without its owners," I said. "And with no way to move onto the next life. How is that not cruel?"

"I didn't think about it that way," she offered with another dismissive shrug.

"You have to give the dog back," I said.

"No way I'm dealing with that crazy chick again. You wanted to know if anyone out there might want to kill me. Well, she's a prime suspect."

"Then you have to give me the jar. I'll give the dog back," I said. "You can't just leave the poor thing in there forever."

"That's why I came here. I knew you'd say that. So, here you go."

Lilith bent down and opened her purse. From it, she produced a small baby food jar.

"I can't believe you did that," I said and set the jar on the mantle. I'd have to open it later. Probably just before I took the dog home.

"Well, I'm here to make it right. That's what matters, right? I wasn't entirely in my right mind there toward the end, and I want to fix things I did wrong."

I blew out a breath. It made me feel better to know that she was at least trying to do the right things. I wished I'd known that old Lilith was slipping enough mentally to put an innocent dog in a jar. I should have known.

We all heard a car pull into the driveway, and Dorian sprang to his feet. "That was fast," he said, thinking it was the Chinese delivery.

Turned out it was Thorn and Jeremy returning from the gun shot call. They booth stepped into the living room and surveyed the little impromptu party.

"We thought you were the Chinese food," Lilith said dryly.

"More takeout?" Thorn asked in the way only Thorn could.

"Chinese delivery," Lilith said before I could speak. "I had a craving and seeing as how I came back from the dead..."

"You want a beer?" Thorn asked Jeremy.

"I'll get it," I said and started to stand up.

"I can get it," Thorn said softly. "I don't want to interrupt."

But I followed him to the kitchen anyway. Jeremy was right behind us, so it was all three of us away from the others. None of them followed.

"So, what happened?" I asked after I got the guys a beer from the fridge.

"Fred was shooting at goats," Thorn said. "So, we had to arrest him."

"That was fast," I said looking at the clock.

"Well, I made the arrest, but one of the other deputies took him in," Thorn followed up.

"Did any of the goats get killed?" I asked as that horrible thought dawned on me. "Did any of them get hurt?"

"No, thankfully, he has bad aim and the goats were small," Thorn answered.

"And thankfully, he didn't hurt anyone else," I said.

"Well, that's why we arrested him. Though, I'm pretty sure those goats were trying to kill him. I told him he couldn't just shoot like that."

"I suggested we call a rescue to round them up," Jeremy added. "They've become a real menace."

"We can't do that, Jeremy," I responded. "They're people. Did Thorn tell you they're people? At some point, we have to change them back, it's just that… it's all so much right now."

"He did fill me in," Jeremy said. "I get why we can't call a rescue, but we're going to have to do something soon. Either the goats are going to get hurt or someone else is."

I sighed and rubbed my temples. "I really want to go to bed," I said.

"Well, then tell your friends and Lilith good night, and go to bed, sweetie. Everyone will understand. You've had a long day. Heck, you've had a few long days."

"Lilith won't understand. Plus, she just ordered Chinese food."

"It's a to-go order. She can take it back to her house. It will be in a bag and everything," Thorn said pragmatically.

"And I'll get my wife and the others," Jeremy said. "If they want to continue the party, we can do it at my house. Otherwise, I'll make sure everyone gets home."

I wanted to protest further, but I was too exhausted. And I wasn't in the right mood to try to use magic to prop myself up artificially.

So, I headed into the living room and found Dorian taking the food from the delivery driver. Apparently, the food arrived while we were in the kitchen.

"You're going to have to take that with you," I said. "I'm sorry, you guys, but I've got to go to bed."

Lilith looked a little upset, but she came over and gave me a hug. "Call me tomorrow?"

"Of course," I said. "I'm going to take the dog back to Druella, and then I'll come by. How about that?"

"Can you bring burgers?"

I laughed. "Yes, I can do that. You're starting to sound like Meri, though."

"Hey, is that supposed to be an insult?" Meri stirred on the sofa. He'd apparently fallen back asleep even though Lilith had gotten up to get her food.

"I would never," I said and feigned innocence.

"Whatever," he groused and went back to snoozing.

After our long Midwestern goodbyes, everyone finally left. Thorn and I trudged up the stairs, and after checking on the girls, went to bed.

I'd barely had the energy to throw on my pajamas, but I made it to the bed. My eyes were closing as soon as my head hit the pillow.

But every hour on the hour, I was woken up by the sound of what could only be bleating goats.

Chapter Nine

"Coffee," I moaned as I walked into the kitchen.

Mom was there getting the girls breakfast before she took them to school. Thorn must have called her when he left for work and told her I had a rough night.

I felt bad for him because how could his have been any better? Of course, he was Thorn and probably hadn't even skipped his morning run.

"What are you up to today?" Mom asked as she put a cup of steaming coffee into my hand.

I took a sip. It was perfect. "Old Lilith put her neighbor's dog in a jar. I'm going to release it and take it back to its owner. Also, hopefully find out if said neighbor hated her enough to kill her."

Hekate giggled.

"It's not funny," I said softly. "I know you look up to Lilith, but we don't hurt innocent animals."

"He's not hurt," Hekate insisted. "He's in a doggy paradise."

Did Lilith have Hekate help her with putting the dog in a jar? "Did you help her with that?" I asked.

"It's fine," Mom said. "This is a fresh start."

I studied her face. I knew she didn't really believe that, but I figured out why she said it without having to ask. She didn't want me getting mad at Hekate for something Lilith did.

"You're right, Mom. But never do that again," I said firmly to Hekate. "I mean it. Shadow work is one thing, but never use it against animals. And if anyone ever tries to get you to do something like that again, then you need to tell me."

"Is Lilith in trouble?" Laney asked before taking another big bite of the waffle Mom had made for her.

"Old Lilith might have been, but Grandma's right. This is a fresh start. Hopefully, if any of us ever start to struggle with our decisions the way old Lilith did, someone will step in to help."

"You guys are sticks in the mud," Hekate said before getting up.

I didn't reply as she took her dish to the sink. I watched her wash the dish and place it in the drying rack.

Hekate went to leave the kitchen, and for a moment, I thought she would walk right past me. But instead, she stopped and looked up into my face. "I would never hurt a dog," she tried to reassure.

"I know that, sweetie," I said and smoothed her dark hair. "And I'll return Druella's dog to her today. The little doggie didn't suffer, so I'm sure it will all be fine."

"I'm going to go finish getting ready," she said with a relieved smile.

Laney washed her dish next and then hugged me wordlessly on her way out of the room. Mom just had coffee which she refilled.

"You need me to go with you? I can come back after I take the girls to school."

"It's all right. I'll already be at her house by then," I replied. "As soon as you're gone with the girls, I'll get the dog out of the jar. I'm sure both the dog and Druella would like for me to delay their reunion as little as possible."

I probably should have waited until I was in the car to get the dog, Spotty, out of the jar. He went absolutely bananas as soon as he was free. Thankfully, Meri was able to communicate with the pooch and calm him considerably.

I didn't have a leash because we didn't own a dog, but he heeled beside me as we walked to the car. I opened the back door and he hopped in obediently.

"Thank you so much," I said to Meri as I buckled into the driver's side. "This would have been an unmitigated disaster without you."

"Wouldn't everything be an unmitigated disaster without me?" Meri groused.

"I guess you're right."

Spotty barked in response. I had to admit his bark was a bit yappy, but that was to be expected from a tiny fluffball. Spotty was a Pomeranian without a single spot.

He reminded me of a dog I'd had once. One that got into a magical potion and ended up with the spirit of a witch possessing them. That little fluffball was now the familiar of one of my Aunties because we could not get the witch out, and after a time, their souls combined.

But that didn't matter. What mattered was that I had Spotty to return to Druella.

The woman was in her front yard pulling weeds from a flowerbed when I pulled into her driveway. She knelt on a flower-patterned cushion. Her straw hat bobbed as she yanked and discarded the errant weeds. As soon as Spotty saw her, he started barking his head off. Druella's head whipped around at the sound so hard her hat nearly came off.

She jumped up from the cushion and rushed to my car. "You've found him!"

Druella mashed tears out of her eyes as she threw my passenger door open, I'd already unlocked it for her, and Spotty leapt into her arms. The little doggy covered her face in kisses.

"Don't even think about it," Meri said as I threw him a look. "I would never debase myself that way."

Thankfully, Druella was too busy with Spotty to notice. The veil would have kept her from noticing anyway. If she lived a couple of doors down from Lilith and couldn't feel her magic, it meant she was dead to it. Some people just had no sensitivity to magic whatsoever.

"You found him," she said again, but upon looking at me closer, she finally realized who I was. "Where was she keeping him?"

Uh… I couldn't tell her that Lilith had put her precious dog in a jar. She wouldn't even have the ability to understand that. So, I had to decide what to say. Technically, Lilith did kidnap her dog… But I couldn't tell Druella that. My loyalty was to my family and my coven first. I was obligated to return the dog but not to sell out Lilith in the process.

"Lilith didn't have Spotty," I lied. "I found him wandering in the woods behind my house. Actually, he came out of the woods into my backyard."

"That's mighty convenient considering the person who I swore stole him died recently. And now here he is with the dognapper's niece returning him."

"I know how it looks," I said. *And you're right.* I didn't say. "But I really did find him. I've brought him back to you. Isn't that what's important?"

She held Spotty up and looked him over thoroughly. Once Druella was satisfied that he wasn't injured in any way, she turned her attention back to me. "I suppose it doesn't matter what I think now. She's dead, and I doubt you had anything to do with Spotty going missing. I don't know how it is you could be related to that woman. I hear good things around town about you, Kinsley, but you and that Lilith were as different as night and day."

I wasn't sure what to say to that. "My aunt had her quirks."

Druella let out a braying laugh. "You could say that! Anyway, I should get Spotty inside and get him some of his favorite treats. Would you like to come inside for some tea or a root beer float?"

It wasn't often I was invited into someone's house for a root beer float. Plus, I still needed to suss out whether Druella had been the one to kill Lilith. I doubted it, but I couldn't leave until I knew for sure. Plus, who could turn down a root beer float?

"Well, I'll take a float if you're having one," I said.

"I know it's early for something so decadent, but I've been out here gardening since sunup. Nothing quite hits the spot like a good float after some gardening in the hot sun."

It wasn't really that hot out, but then again, I hadn't been gardening. And who was I to argue with ice cream and soda?

"It sounds good to me. I haven't had one in forever," I said as I followed Druella into her house.

"That cat well behaved?" she asked and nodded toward Meri. "I'd hate to just leave him outside."

"He's a perfect gentleman," I answered. "Well trained."

"Well, bring him in then. Spotty here likes cats."

"Come on, Meri," I said and then whistled like he was a dog. I knew that would annoy him, but he scowled at me and then came running.

"I'll fix a dish of ice cream for them too, if that's okay?" Druella said as she shut the door behind me. "Spotty loves a small scoop. I figure as long as his weight stays in the healthy range, a treat every now and then doesn't hurt."

"I don't think Meri likes ice cream," I said and winked at Meri.

He let out a distraught meowl.

"I'm kidding," I said and chuckled. "I'm sure he'd love that. Thank you."

"So weird. It's almost like he knew what you were saying," she said and tutted. "Oh, well. I'm going to go make the ice cream. Come on into the kitchen and have a seat."

I sat down at Druella's kitchen table and watched her retrieve ice cream from her freezer and cans of root beer from her fridge. "You don't want diet, do you?" she asked. "I think I've got a can or two for when my mom visits if you do."

"No, regular is fine," I said and shivered at the thought of a diet root beer float.

She scooped ice cream into two small bowls using what looked like a cookie scoop. After setting the dishes on the floor for Spotty and Meri, she put the tiny scoop in the sink and grabbed a bigger one from a drawer.

A couple of minutes later, Druella joined me at the table with two floats. She'd put them in actual soda fountain glasses, the tall kind with edges bowed out like a flower.

"Oh, I forgot the straws."

Druella hopped up from her chair and retrieved two bright pink straws from her pantry. She plopped one into my float and then one into hers before sitting down again.

I took a sip and thought about how to ask her for her alibi on the morning Lilith died. As the cool, sugary concoction hit my tongue, I realized there probably wasn't a polite way to broach the subject. How do you ask your host if they killed their neighbor while sitting in their kitchen drinking their root beer and eating their ice cream?

"You've got something on your mind," Druella pulled me out of my thoughts. Her pale blue eyes studied me for a moment. "You think I had something to do with her death."

"I don't want to sit at your kitchen table and make accusations like that," I said. "But I was wondering how much you hated her? I mean, you thought she stole your dog and did gawd knows what with him."

"Well, I suppose I shouldn't be too insulted by that. I mean, if you really thought I poisoned her, you probably wouldn't be sitting here with me drinking my root beer float," Druella said with a dry chuckle.

"I saw you open the can of root beer," I said offhand even though that wasn't really the point. "And you gave me and Spotty ice cream from the same container."

"You're a bright young woman," Druella said with a wistful smile. "I like you, so I won't get mad that you are technically sitting here accusing me of murder. What I will tell you is that on the morning your Auntie died, I was at the mall walking with my usual group. They can all tell you that I wasn't even in town when Lilith died."

"The mall in the city?" It was a dumb question because what other mall?

"Yeah, it's only a twenty-minute drive, and we like to walk inside three days a week. Plus, there's a coffee shop where we can get a coffee and pastries or a sandwich when we're done."

"Who walks with you?" I tried to sound casual.

Druella seemed to think it over for a bit. I wondered what that was about, but before I could ponder it too deeply, she said, "It's me, Mindy Ferguson, Pinky Marple, and Diana Schlepp. But if you're thinking of asking them about my alibi, I'd talk to Pinky. She works at the craft store on the days we don't walk. Mindy is in Aruba with her husband the rest of the week, and Diana works at the hospital."

145

"Pinky works at Sew Crafty?"

"Yep. Just part-time. She mostly does it for the discount on yarn. Apparently knitting can be an expensive habit… I mean hobby. But who am I to talk? Gardening isn't exactly cheap."

"We started a garden," I said. "My daughters, my mom and I. I think my Mom and the girls spend more time gardening than me, though. I have work and… anyway."

Druella smiled at me. "And hunting down killers."

I just stared at her blinking.

That elicited a laugh. "Your husband is the sheriff around these parts, but you've got quite the reputation for solving crime. Plus, running two businesses. I can only imagine that you don't have a ton of time for gardening. I love your donuts, by the way. Best I've ever had. So much better than that schlock you get at the grocery store."

"Thank you," I said. "That really means a lot to me." I opened my purse and pulled out a couple of donut coupons that I carried around for just such occasions. "Here, these will get you a couple of free donuts. My way of saying thank you for the root beer floats and for not getting angry about the topic of conversation."

I liked Druella. Maybe she was just being nice to me because I returned her beloved dog, but I hoped that new Lilith would be nicer to her.

"Oh, thank you! Normally I'd tell you that it's not necessary to pay me back for the floats, but I'm not going to turn down free donuts."

Just then, my phone rang, and I saw it was Craft Donuts. "I have to take this," I said. "I'm sorry."

"Go ahead. I'll just wash up the dishes."

It was Chalfy, my manager at Craft Donuts, letting me know that Bergamot had a flat tire. And that there were too many people around for her to use magic to fix it, so she either had to wait for them to disperse or change the flat. Either way, she was running late and the shop was swamped.

"I'll be there in five minutes," I said and hung up.

"Everything okay?" Druella asked.

"Yep. Just need to get into Craft Donuts. They're swamped and they need me."

"I'm not surprised you're so busy. Well, thank you for the visit and for bringing Spotty back to me. I've been a mess without him."

"You are most welcome. And maybe we should do this again soon," I said sensing that she didn't really want me to leave.

I could feel other people's emotions sometimes, and Druella was lonely. She had Spotty back, and her walking group, but I sensed that she didn't get many visitors. And she liked visitors.

"That would be lovely. Drop by anytime for a root beer float."

"I will do just that."

I picked up Meri and we headed out to the car. My next stop was my donut shop to cover for my perpetually late, but very loveable so I couldn't fathom firing her, employee.

Chapter Ten

I was only at Craft Donuts for about an hour before Bergamot showed up, and right when she clocked in, the rush started to die off. I tended to a couple of things in my office, but after that, there wasn't much reason for me to stay.

Since I still had several hours before the girls got out of school, I decided to go see a woman about craft supplies and an alibi for Druella. I wanted to just believe her, but I decided to check it out anyway. Grief could blind a person, and I didn't want to let Lilith's killer slip through my fingers because I liked root beer floats.

"I'm going to head out, guys," I said to Chalfy and Bergamot.

They were both behind the counter waiting for a customer, who was bent over looking in the glass cases, to decide which donuts they wanted in his dozen. Once the guy stood up and said he was ready, Bergamot stepped forward to finish his order.

Chalfy turned to me and said, "Are you doing okay? We've been worried about you."

"I'm doing fine," I said with a smile.

Chalfy recoiled a bit, and I realized that maybe he didn't know about Lilith? That almost seemed impossible.

"You know that she's back, right?" I asked.

"I heard, but we weren't sure if it was true. Bergamot thought maybe it was just a rumor. But it's true? She's really back? And younger?"

"It's all true. She really is back, and she really seems to be about eighty years younger." I kept my voice down.

While the veil would keep people from hearing what I was saying, there was no reason to make it work overtime. Or risk a customer with some level of sensitivity hearing what I was saying and freaking out.

"Well, I'm glad for you guys," Chalfy said as another customer came into the shop. "I'm going to get back to work. Call me if you need anything, boss."

"You do the same."

I left the shop but decided to stop at the Brew Station before I went to Sew Crafty. I wanted a coffee and to say hi to Viv.

She was behind the counter wiping it down when I walked in. Viv had employees to do the grunt work around the coffee shop, but she seemed to enjoy doing a lot of it herself. "Time to lean is time to clean," she'd say to the playful eyeroll of her dedicated employees. They all loved her because she really only held herself to that standard. Of course, being a hard-working and caring boss made her employees want to work hard for her.

"Oh, hey, Kinsley," Viv said as I approached the counter. She stowed the cleaning rag and spray bottle under the counter. "Let me wash my hands and then what can I get for you?"

"Just my usual. To go, please. I'm heading over to Sew Crafty."

"Cool," she said over her shoulder as she washed her hands at the sink on the back wall behind the counter. "Are you taking up a new hobby?"

I looked around before speaking. There was only one customer in the shop, and he was seated by the window. He also had earbuds in and seemed to be engrossed in something on his laptop.

"I'm actually going there to check on the alibi of one of Lilith's neighbors," I said.

"The one with the dog?" Viv asked.

"Yeah. Her name is Druella, and I don't think she did it, but I wouldn't feel right about not following up."

"That sounds smart. Let me get your drink so you can be on your way."

"Thanks," I said and put a five-dollar bill in the tip jar while I waited.

When Viv was done, she slid my to-go cup across the counter to me. Her eyes and the corners of her mouth were stretched with strain.

"What is it?" I asked.

"Well, I didn't want to bother you with this, but earlier today, I heard something. A man who works at the courthouse, and who comes in everyday for coffee and a breakfast sandwich, was talking to another customer about Lilith. And the topic of the conversation had me wondering. I wasn't even sure about mentioning it now. You know with Lilith being back and all."

"Who?" I asked. "What were they talking about?"

"Lilith was being sued. I mean, the case is dropped because she's technically dead. But the owner of Mr. John's Diner sued her for saying that she found roaches in her grilled cheese sandwich."

"You can't sue someone for that," I said and took a sip of my coffee. "Besides, it was probably true. That place was a dive. The only people who ate there were drunks and truck drivers, and even the truck drivers stopped going there."

"Well, Mr. John says that the reason people stopped going there was because of her and her roach comments."

"That's ridiculous. People are allowed to have opinions about restaurants."

"Yeah, but the lawsuit alleges that she was shouting her opinion outside the diner. And Mr. John sued because he said it was enough to destroy his business."

"I can't believe I didn't hear about this," I said. "You'd think the rumor mill would have been achurnin' about that kind of gossip."

"The judge ordered them not to talk about it," Viv said. "At least, that's what the guy at the courthouse said. And think about it. Lilith probably didn't think it was a big deal, right? And Mr. John probably wanted nothing more than for people to stop talking about it. So, he wasn't going to fuel the gossip."

"I suppose," I said and sipped my coffee. "Well, I was going to go over to Sew Crafty, but since I really don't think Druella did it, I guess I should stop in at Mr. John's."

"If you get anything to eat, make sure you ask for it without the extra crunchies," Viv said with a chuckle.

"Oh, that's mean," I said but couldn't help my smile. "Lilith has rubbed off on both of us."

"Catch you later, Kinsley."

I said goodbye and headed out to my car. The last place I wanted to go was Mr. John's. I didn't mind diners. In fact, when I first came back to Coventry, the diner Reggie worked at was one of my family's favorite places to eat.

But Mr. John's was a different story. It sat on the outskirts of town, past Mann's, next to a dilapidated old gas station. Nobody knew how either establishment stayed in business.

You had to drive right past Mann's to get to the older gas station, and Mann's was much cleaner and brighter. Plus, there wasn't a crotchety old man running the place to act like you were a burden. And as far as Mr. John's Diner went, well, let's just say Lilith wasn't the first person to point out that sometimes your meal came with a side of "extra crunchies."

The real mystery was why she was there eating grilled cheese in the first place? The only answer I could come up with was that it was on the way out to the farm where Lilith was supposedly blackmailing the farmer into letting her grow dangerous or illegal plants. That was another lead I needed to follow up on, but it seemed to be the most serious, so I guessed I was saving it for last.

Talking to the farmer was like my main quest, and I kept getting distracted with side quests. Speaking of side quests, I was still sitting behind the wheel of my car, sipping my latte, when I realized I didn't even know if Mr. John had a reason to kill Lilith.

What if he was winning the lawsuit? Then killing her wouldn't have been necessary, right? But then again, what if winning the lawsuit wasn't enough for him? What if he'd been so angry that only her death would quench his rage?

I had a choice to make. Did I go into the courthouse and try to find out the details of the lawsuit? Or did I go straight to Mr. John's?

And then a thought hit me. If Lilith was being sued, then she probably had all of the paperwork. Even if she said she couldn't remember anything about it, which would most likely be a lie, she'd still have all of the court filings.

All I had to do was go to her house and ask for them. I could figure out if the case was going her way or his. But then either way, he still might have wanted to kill her.

So, I put the car in gear and headed out toward Mr. John's. "Where are we going?" a voice startled me from the backseat of the car.

"Meri! You scared the bejeezus out of me!"

"Only because you forgot me in the car," he snarked.

"I didn't forget you in the car," I said, but I had sort of forgotten that he'd stayed in the car napping, with the climate control on, while I was in Craft Donuts working.

"Whatever," he said and stretched before hopping onto the console. "Where are we going?"

"We're going to Mr. John's Diner."

"Pass," Meri said. "Not even bacon is worth that."

See. It wasn't just Lilith.

"We're not going there to eat. Mr. John was suing Lilith for destroying his business."

"Wow. Well, he was doing that all on his own, but okay," Meri said as he curled up in the passenger side. "When we're done accusing townsfolk of murder, can we stop somewhere good to eat?"

"I'm pretty sure that we'll need to go home."

"Why?"

"I have daughters," I said with a chuckle. "They're going to get out of school at some point."

"So, text your mom and have her watch them. I want a burger."

"Meri, I'm not having my mother babysit the girls just so you can have a burger. She already got them ready for school this morning and took them. She'll pick them up too, but then I want them home with me. Mom needs free time too."

"She likes it."

"That's not the point, Meri."

"I think it is."

"You don't think."

"Whatever."

"We're here," I said as I pulled into the mostly abandoned Mr. John's parking lot.

There was just one other car. It was an ancient hatchback that appeared to be held together with duct tape and prayers. At one time, probably ten years before, it had most likely been red. Time had turned it to a sort of faded pinkish orange, and one of the tires was half flat. Meri barely glanced at the car through my open driver's side door and then asked me to make sure I locked the doors.

"Do you want to come in with me?" I asked.

"I doubt they allow cats in this fine dining establishment," he said and curled up in the passenger seat.

"And I doubt there's even anybody here to care. It looks like the only person here is the one person working…"

"Maybe the employees got rides. I'm fine. Just holler or something if you get in trouble."

"You do the same," I said.

"I don't think I'll need any help."

"You're the one who's afraid of a hatchback," I said and slammed the car door shut before he could respond.

As soon as I turned around, the smell of stale grease assaulted my nose. That odor told you that anything fried you ordered would taste like overused oil. It was a real shame because fried foods were usually the best part of greasy spoons.

I made my way quickly across the lot. It wasn't that hot of a day, but without any trees, the sun was glaring up at me from the bare asphalt. The parking lot felt twenty degrees hotter than it had inside Coventry, and it wasn't helping the stale grease smell.

My stomach churned right as I pushed the dirty, broken door of the diner open. "Sit anywhere you want," was shouted gruffly at me from somewhere in the kitchen.

As I'd expected, there was no one else around. I didn't see anyone behind the counter or any waitresses. If there was only one person working, I assumed it was Mr. John himself, but I'd have to confirm that. You'd have thought if his business was struggling that much, he'd try a little harder to provide good customer service.

But he did not, and five minutes later, I was still standing there by the counter waiting for him to emerge from the kitchen. When the faded red door between the front of house and kitchen finally swung open, the man who'd yelled at me earlier appraised me with skeptical annoyance.

"I ain't buying anything. If you ain't a customer, move along."

As if he could afford to be rude. To kick people out…

"I'm not here to eat," I said and looked around.

The truth was that I wouldn't even want to sit down. I'd stood by the counter and tried not to touch anything. The whole place looked, and smelled, like it was covered in a layer of grime. Lilith was such a

159

weirdo for walking into that place, sitting down, and actually staying long enough to order food.

"Then move along. I ain't got time for shenanigans."

How could he not have time? What else could he possibly be doing? He owned a diner with no diners. On second thought, I didn't want to know…

"I do want to talk to you, though," I said and didn't move from my spot on the dingy black and white linoleum floor.

"Talk is cheap," he said and waved me off.

"You were suing my great-aunt," I said and that stopped him in his tracks.

Mr. John, who I confirmed was Mr. John by his response to my statement, said, "You're related to that crazy old bat?"

"If by 'crazy old bat,' you mean my Great-Aunt Lilith, then yes. We're related."

"What do you want?" he asked but didn't tell me to leave again. "You inheriting any money from her? I could sue you. Er, her estate as it were."

Ah, so that's why he didn't tell me to get out. I could almost see the dollar signs dancing in his cold, desperate eyes.

Mr. John would never get a dime from my family, but I could use it as leverage. Maybe if he thought he could sue me, and not end up in a jar on my fireplace mantle, he might let some information slip.

"I don't know anything about an inheritance," I said. "I'm not sure that my aunt had any money when she died."

"Oh, don't feed me that bull. I know all about her finances and that big fancy house she lived in too. Maybe the judge will give me that big fancy house in my lawsuit."

That almost made me chuckle. Lilith would destroy this man. Probably the only reason he was still standing was that she really hadn't cared about his stupid lawsuit.

Unless he killed her. But something I hadn't thought of before I drove all the way out to his crappy diner was how he would have gotten to her.

"Were you at my aunt's house the morning she died?" I asked bluntly.

That would have been the only way he could have gotten to her, after all. If he'd showed up after I left to harass her. Or perhaps to pretend he was going to drop the lawsuit. Would Lilith have let him in because she figured she could toy with him?

"Why would I be at that crazy bi… woman's house?"

That I didn't know. But what I did know was that answering a question with a question was a form of deflection. Why hadn't he just answered me?

"You didn't answer my question," I said. "Were you at her house that morning or weren't you?"

"Why would I be? I'm not answering because you're not making any dang sense."

"Maybe you were losing the lawsuit," I offered. "Or maybe you were winning, but getting her money wasn't enough. Maybe you wanted her to pay for ruining your diner with more than cash."

"You are all crazy," he said, and I noticed that his voice had gotten louder. "Did you really drive all the way out here to accuse me of murder?"

"Well, I didn't drive out here for the food," I said and then covered my mouth.

I hadn't meant to actually say that part out loud. I watched as Mr. John's face turned bright red and then just kept going right on to purple.

He was about to blow his top, and he still hadn't answered my question. His eyes flicked to the right, and I followed.

Much to my shock, there was a huge knife on the counter next to a dirty dishrag. Was he planning on lunging for it?

I would never know. The pathetic bells over the broken door let out a clang as someone walked into the diner. I turned around and saw Thorn standing there. He put his hands on his hips and gave me a look.

"Kinsley, what are you doing here?"

Chapter Eleven

"Thorn, hi," I said and retreated to stand next to him. "What are you doing here?"

And there it was. I'd done the exact same thing Mr. John was doing. I'd answered Thorn's question with a question, but the difference was, Thorn would know I was deflecting.

But what did I have to be defensive about? It's not like he was investigating Lilith's death. I was doing exactly what I was supposed to be doing.

But before I could say any of that, Thorn spoke again. "I was on my way to a call and saw your car in the parking lot. You don't usually eat here, so I thought I'd drop in and make sure everything is okay."

"If the two of you aren't going to order anything, please leave. I'm a busy man," Mr. John said.

I still couldn't figure out what he'd be busy doing...

"Come on," Thorn said and opened the door of the diner for me.

I thought about protesting, but why? I wasn't going to get anything out of Mr. John. I was beginning to feel like going there at all was a silly idea.

Thorn walked me to my car. He'd parked right by me, but before I got in, he pulled me in for a kiss.

"What was that for?" I asked when we parted. "Not that I mind."

He chuckled. "You had that look on your face when we were walking out here."

"What look?"

"The one where you think I'm going to chide you for being here. I just wanted to let you know that I was genuinely curious about why you're here. I wasn't here to police your behavior."

"Then why did you drag me out of there?" I asked.

He laughed a hearty belly laugh. "I didn't drag you out of there, Kinsley. I opened the door and said, 'come on.' Did you still need to talk to him?" Concern etched his face as his eyes narrowed and his forehead scrunched up a little.

"I don't. If you'd chided me for coming here, you'd have been right. But don't ever do that," I said and poked his arm playfully. "I'm not a child. I don't need to be scolded."

"I know that," Thorn said and crossed his arms over his chest. His biceps reflected the work he'd been putting into them, and I wished he'd pull me in for another kiss. "We'll go back in if you want."

"No, like I said. It's silly. He would have had to go to Lilith's house, get invited inside, and then sneak poison into her drink without her noticing. I didn't think it through before I came out here. It's just that he had motive, and I also can't figure out why Lilith would eat here."

"She was a little unusual," Thorn said as if that explained everything, and it sort of did…

"What are you doing out here? You said you had a call, but it must not be urgent?"

"The thing with Wayde Barlow has been eating at me," Thorn admitted.

"The farmer who Lilith was allegedly blackmailing," I said. "The one who she was probably 'visiting' when she stopped here at Mr. Johns for the infamous grilled cheese," I said and put the "visiting" part in air quotes with my fingers.

"Yeah," Thorn said and uncrossed his arms. He leaned against his cruiser.

"I thought you weren't investigating Lilith's death since she's alive and the medical examiner ruled it a suicide."

"I'm not investigating her murder. Technically, I'm investigating her blackmailing Wayde Barlow."

"Oh," I said.

"I just figured if it helped you out, then I should do it. I feel pretty useless in this whole thing."

"You're not useless."

"Yeah, but I feel it. I mean, it's Lilith. She's family, and I don't like that my hands are tied because of the ME's ruling. So I was going to do what I could to help. You hadn't mentioned talking to Barlow yet, so I figured I'd mosey on out there. But then I saw your car here. I really was curious."

"Well, this was a bust, but why don't I go with you to talk to Wayde Barlow? We make a pretty good team," I said and poked him in the arm again. Mostly, I was being playful, but I was also marveling at the chiseled heft of his arms.

Nothing wrong with crushing on your husband…

"He won't talk to me if you're there," Thorn said and broke my ogling.

I looked up into his deep, blue eyes. They crinkled a little around the edges when he smiled at me.

"Why wouldn't he talk to you if I'm there?" I asked absently.

"Kinsley, are you all right?" One side of Thorn's mouth cocked up in a lazy half-grin.

"I'm all right," I said and shook my head. "Sorry, it's just that kiss…"

"I guess I don't kiss you like that often enough."

"No, you don't," I protested.

"I'll make a note of it," he said and winked at me. "Sorry, babe. I wish I could take the rest of the day off and kiss you all afternoon, but I'm short a deputy. I've got to stay for my shift."

"Well, then I guess we should go talk to Wayde Barlow," I said, but then my head cleared a little. "Oh, right. He won't talk with me around because I'm Lilith's great-niece. I get it."

"I'll report back to you right away with anything I learn," Thorn offered.

"No need. I can still go," I asserted. "I'll just stay down."

"What?"

"I'll stay down. When you pull up to the farm, I scrunch down and hide in the car. He won't know I'm there."

Thorn looked at me with concern.

"Don't look at me like that. I'm not crazy."

"Said every crazy person ever," he joked, but before I could protest, he pulled me in for another long kiss.

"That's not fair," I said when we finally parted.

"Come on, Kinsley. Let's go. If you want to scrunch down in the car, then you're more than welcome to come along," Thorn said and opened the passenger side of his cruiser for me.

"Let me get Meri," I said and opened my driver's side door to let Meri out.

"Oh, good, the cat's coming too."

The drive to Wayde Barlow's farm was short. He only lived a mile or so away from Mr. John's Diner.

Fortunately, while it was outside of Coventry's town limits, it was still close enough to the ley line that I could draw some power. I'd use magic to amplify my hearing and eavesdrop on Thorn and Wayde's conversation. And then I'd have an excuse to stop and get gyros on the way home. I suddenly found myself craving them big time.

As promised, when Thorn turned onto the long, winding driveway that led up to the Barlow Farm, I scrunched down in my seat. It was wickedly uncomfortable made more so by Thorn laughing at me.

But he redeemed himself by reminding me that I could put the seat back a couple of inches and give myself more room. There wasn't a ton of room because of the metal divider between the front and back seats, but there was enough that it no longer felt like my spleen was in my throat.

"You sure you don't want me to take you back to your car?" Thorn asked as he stopped the cruiser and cut the motor.

"I'm fine," I croaked out.

"I'll be as quick as I can," he said and smoothed the hair on my forehead.

"Don't worry about me. Just get the information," I said.

Thorn got out of the car, and at least that gave me room to lean to the side. I had to stretch myself over his computer and console gear without wrecking everything, but I managed to give myself some breathing room.

I strained my ears to hear, and Meri, who had been at my feet, hopped up into my lap. When I focused my intention on being able to hear what was said on the porch, little tendrils of white light snaked out from my ears and made their way to Thorn. Of course, I was the only one who could see them.

Well, Meri and I. He purred steadily in my lap and amplified my magic. Pretty soon, I heard the sound when Thorn rang the Barlow's doorbell.

And then I heard his wife answer the door. She told Thorn that Wayde wasn't home before asking if he was in any trouble. He reassured her that he was not and asked when Wayde would return.

He was out in the fields, and she didn't know for sure. Most likely it would be sometime around dark.

"Do you want me to call him? I can have him come back. If he'll answer. He doesn't always when he's working," Mrs. Barlow said.

"No, it's okay. It's not urgent. I'll catch him another time," Thorn answered.

"Are you sure he's not in trouble?" she insisted.

"I'm positive, ma'am. I'd tell you more, but it's part of an active investigation," Thorn lied, and I was impressed. He was normally such a straight arrow. "But I can assure you he is not the target of the investigation. I'm just looking for some information."

"Is it maybe something I can help you with?" she asked.

I listened to the silence as Thorn thought it over. I could almost hear those thoughts. Perhaps Mrs. Barlow didn't know about the blackmail. The best way to get someone to refuse to talk to you was to get them in trouble with their wife.

"No, ma'am. I need to speak to Wayde. But please don't worry yourself. I assure you he isn't in any trouble."

They said their goodbyes, and Thorn made his way back to the cruiser. I cut off my spell, and Meri jumped back to the floor where he curled up at my feet.

"Well, that didn't really go anywhere," Thorn said as he started the car.

"You realize she's probably going to grill him when he comes home, and Wayde's not going to have any idea why," I said as Thorn turned his cruiser around and headed down the driveway.

"Oh, I'm sure he'll know, Kinsley. If Lilith was blackmailing him, and now she's dead, then he knows why I stopped by. It will be interesting to see what he does or what he says when I come back," Thorn said.

And then he had a call come in for a disturbance. Thorn dropped me off at my car and headed out to finish his workday.

I still had some time before I needed to get the girls, so I decided to pay Pinky a visit at Sew Crafty. I was curious to see what Wayde Barlow would say, but again, I wasn't sure how he could have gotten to Lilith.

Doubt began to creep into my mind as I drove towards the craft store. How could anybody get close to her? My mind started turning over family again, and I hated that. But honestly, who could have poisoned her but... me?

I shook my head to clear those thoughts as I turned into the Sew Crafty parking lot. That type of thinking wasn't productive at all, and I knew nobody thought it was me... right?

The best thing for me to do was just keep my head down and keep moving forward with the investigation. I was already at Sew Crafty, so all I needed to do was pop in and have Pinky confirm that Druella was at the mall with her when Lilith died.

Meri was curled up in the passenger seat sleeping, so I set the climate control for him and left him to his nap. Though I doubted he would have been unwelcome at Sew Crafty. A witch owned the store. But he seemed to have zero interest in going with me.

Typical.

Once I walked past the automatic doors and into the store, Pinky wasn't hard to find. She lived up to her name. Though the roots of her hair were a silvery gray, and desperately needed a touchup, the rest of her hair was a shock of electric pink. She was in the yarn aisle putting skeins of colorful yarn into their respective bins. Every few seconds, she would take a piece of candy from the pocket of her orange smock and pop it in her mouth.

"Pinky?" I asked as I approached.

When she turned to face me, her name tag confirmed I'd been correct. "Can I help you?" she asked before shoving a dark purple skein of yarn into its bin.

"I hope so," I said. "Uh, my name is Kinsley Wilson."

"Did you need help finding something, Kinsley Wilson?" And then I knew she was a witch. And one of the ones in town who were not a huge fan of my family or coven.

Why they stayed in Coventry, I had no idea. But as long as they didn't challenge us or make trouble, I had no reason to run them out either. Sure, they talked crap about us, but a little bad-mouthing never actually hurt anyone.

"I'm here to ask you about Druella," I said plainly.

"What about her?" Pinky shot back.

"I'm sure you heard that my Great-Aunt Lilith died recently…"

"You could call it that," she said and looked around. "Though I guess she didn't really stay that way, did she?"

I nodded my head. "But the fact remains that someone tried to hurt her."

"Lot of people wanted her hurt," Pinky said. "From what I hear. Look, I'm no saint, but some of the stuff that witch messed around with made a lot of folks uncomfortable."

"Like who?" I asked and suddenly wondered if Pinky was more than just a rival witch.

She waved her hand dismissively. "Nothing specific that I can recall. She just turned a lot of heads."

"Like yours?"

"Look, I was at the mall walking with some of the girls the day she died. You can ask around. I've got nothing to hide."

"But what about Druella?" I countered. "That's why I'm here, after all. She said she was walking with you that morning and that you could alibi her."

Pinky thought it over a bit longer than I expected. "She stood us up that morning."

"What?" I was a little dumbfounded.

I'd fully expected Pinky to alibi Druella, and then I'd just move on to a better suspect. Pinky revealing that Druella was lying was a bit of a shock.

"You came here to ask me if she was with us, and I'm telling you she was not. She texted me to tell me that morning that she wasn't feeling well. I can show you the text if you want."

"Please," I said.

Pinky sighed and pulled her phone from her apron. She woke it up and started scrolling. "Drat. Well, I erased her texts when I blocked her."

"You blocked her?" It was unfortunate because that text would have moved Druella up to the top of my suspect list. Without seeing it, I didn't know what to think.

"Yeah, Druella has been… a nuisance lately. We just didn't want that negativity in the group anymore."

"A nuisance how?"

"You know. Just needy and overly emotional. It was bringing down the vibe of the group."

"Someone stole her dog," I offered curtly. "She was sad."

Pinky waved me off. "I get it, but the walking group is a way for us to raise our vibrations. We're trying to be on a positive frequency with the Universe."

"And you did that by ditching a friend who was going through a rough patch?"

"Don't judge me," she half snarled. "It was Lilith who stole her dog. Everybody knows it, so what room do you have to talk?"

"Well, if you say that Druella wasn't with you the morning my Auntie died, then I think we're done here," I said.

"I guess we are," Pinky retorted with a shrug.

Chapter Twelve

My next stop was Druella's house. While I didn't like or trust Pinky, I had to know if Druella had just lied to me. And why? Why would she do that if she knew it was just going to come back and bite her in the butt? None of it made sense, and I knew I wouldn't be able to let it go until I sorted the mess out.

As soon as she answered her door, she could tell something was up. "Oh, no," she said with a resigned sigh. "I was hoping she would be the bigger person and just tell you the truth."

"So, you know why I'm here," I said.

"Because Pinky told you I wasn't with them that morning," Druella answered. "Come in," she said and stepped back so I could step over the threshold.

It occurred to me that once again, I could be stepping into the house of the person who tried to take out Lilith. But my curiosity overrode any potential hesitation.

"Why did you send me to talk to her if you knew she might not alibi you?" I asked.

"Because I've been friends with those women for years. We had a falling out. Unkind words were said, but I never thought she'd actually let me go down for murder. Not over a stupid squabble," Druella said before grinding a tear out of her eye with her knuckle. "I'm sorry. I don't mean to get emotional. I'm glad Spotty is back because it appears that without him, I'd be friendless."

"I'm so sorry," I said. "But I have to ask… were you really with them?"

"I was. I swear!" Druella insisted.

"Maybe if I asked one of the other women?"

"No. That won't work. It's the reason I sent you to Pinky in the first place. She's kind of the group leader. I guess that's what you'd call it."

"The head mean girl?"

"I guess she is," Druella admitted. "It's so funny. Not in a comical way. But we're basically old women, and they still act like we're in high school. Anyway, by now, Pinky has told the other two not to talk to you. Or she's told them what to say. They won't cross her."

"Okay," I took a deep breath. "I believe you," I said, and I mostly did.

"What are you going to do?" she asked.

"Right now, I'm going to go home. My girls are going to be getting out of school soon, and I want to spend the afternoon with them before I make my family dinner."

"That sounds wonderful," Druella said wistfully.

I felt a pang of guilt about her loneliness. Not that it was my fault, but I still felt bad for her. So, on impulse, I said, "Do you want to join us?"

Her eyes lit up for a moment. "Oh, I would, but I have a couple of appointments this afternoon. And then I volunteered to work at the soup kitchen in the city. I figured it was better than sitting around alone."

"Well, another time, then."

"That would be lovely. Maybe I could give you and your girls some garden pointers."

"We would love that."

And then we said our goodbyes. After the conversation, I felt almost sure that Druella had nothing to do with Lilith's demise, but I still felt the niggle of need to know for sure.

It weighed heavily on my mind until I got home. Mom had already planned on picking up the girls from school, so I texted her that she could bring them right over once she had them.

While I waited for them, I made an after-school snack. Oh, and bacon for Meri.

He waited patiently at me feet as I fried it in a pan. He got a lot of heated up precooked bacon, but I had some time, so I made him some real pan-fried stuff. His tail swished happily as I flipped the slices with tongs.

"Meri, you are so good about not getting on the counters," I said as we waited the last couple of minutes of cooking time.

"I wouldn't want to get squirted with a water bottle," he groused.

"I have never," I protested.

"I wouldn't put it past you, though."

"I'm offended."

"You're something," he retorted. "Anyway, I don't get on the counters because I'm not some basic cat."

"You get on the kitchen table," I pointed out.

"But you invite me to do that. Besides, it's only my front paws so I can eat. I can sit on the floor."

"No, that's fine. I don't want you to have to eat on the floor."

Once Meri had his mountain of bacon, I set to making a snack for the girls…and me. I didn't want to ruin our dinner, not that that was ever a problem, but

I thought grilled cheese and creamy tomato soup sounded good.

So, I made grilled cheese with three kinds of cheese, provolone, cheddar, and muenster, and then cut the sandwiches into strips for better dipping. After that, I heated up some organic tomato soup in a pan on the stove, and I added some heavy cream. I whisked it together perfectly and then poured it into soup mugs just as I heard my mom pull into the driveway.

The girls ran into the house with Mom in tow. They took their shoes off and put their backpacks in the dining room.

"That smells so good," Mom said as she wandered into the kitchen.

"Do you want some? I made plenty," I said as I realized I hadn't put soup in a mug for her.

"No, that's all right. Since I'm dropping the girls off with you, your dad wants to run some errands. Thank you for the offer, though."

Mom left to run Dad's errands, and the girls and I sat around the kitchen table eating our snack and talking about our days. Well, the girls talked about their days. I left most of mine out.

"I have homework," Laney said.

"Me too," Hekate followed up. "Well, it's just seeds. I'm supposed to put them in a wet paper towel and put it in the window to sprout."

"I can help you with that," I said. "And then I thought we could do some gardening?"

"But my homework?" Laney said sadly. You could tell she really wanted to garden, but her responsibility ate at her. She always liked to get her homework done right away.

"Why don't we do our gardening, and then Daddy can help you with your homework after dinner?" I said, and she brightened.

"You think he would?" she asked hopefully.

"Well, is it magic homework or mundane stuff?"

"Math," she rolled her eyes. Responsible or not, math was not exciting.

Except to Thorn. "I'm pretty sure he'd love to help you with your math homework," I said. "Is it a lot?"

"It's, like, ten problems."

"Oh, yeah, you guys can knock that out right after dinner."

"What are we having for dinner?" Hekate asked as she dipped her last piece of grilled cheese in the remnants of her soup.

183

"Oh, is that grilled cheese?!" Bonkers asked as he stumbled into the kitchen.

"It is," I answered. "And I saved you some. But where were you?"

"There was something in the tree out front. I wanted to check it out," Bonkers answered.

"Something?"

"About that grilled cheese?" Bonkers answered.

I wasn't sure if he didn't want to tell me what was in the haunted tree in our front yard or if he'd immediately forgotten what we were talking about. Either way, I got up, put my dishes in the sink, and cut his strips of grilled cheese into tiny bite-sized pieces.

Meri looked at me mournfully as I set Bonkers' plate on the floor. "Where's mine?"

"Since when do you eat grilled cheese?" I asked. "Plus, you just had bacon. I didn't save any for you."

"Lies. You told Brighton you had plenty, and I can see an entire grilled cheese sandwich on that plate," he said and nodded toward the counter.

"Fine, I didn't want to cut up another sandwich just to give you a couple of pieces, but I will," I said.

"I'll take the rest," Hekate volunteered.

"Okay. You okay? You're very hungry this afternoon. Maybe you're going to have a growth spurt."

"They had chicken legs at lunch," she said with a shrug. "I don't really like them."

"Ah, okay. Well, you can have the rest of the sandwich. We'll make sure we have a filling dinner too. Tater tot casserole?"

"Yay!" Laney said. She got up and put her dishes in the sink. "I mean, I'm not as hungry, but I still like the tater tot casserole."

"Did you guys have chicken legs too?" I asked Laney.

"We did, but I like them. Plus, my friend Amalee doesn't like them, so I got hers too."

Once everyone was done with their snack, we washed the grease from the grilled cheese off our hands in preparation to get them dirty with dirt. Everyone filed outside to the backyard, and Bonkers found himself a shady spot under a tree off the patio.

The girls, Meri, and I walked out to the garden and I opened the gate. Our garden was inside an ornate wrought iron fence, and all of the plants were growing in raised beds. Well, Laney had planted a few vegetables on the ground for bunnies and ground hogs. We'd planted our stuff in the raised beds to keep the critters out, but she thought that was unfair.

Laney began pulling weeds while Hekate tended to her "tomato" plant. It was actually a belladonna, and she thought I didn't know, but I knew. Lilith must have given her the seed. I'd been debating for some time what to do about it, but so far, I'd just let it go. It was locked behind a gate, and she only came out to tend to it when I was around.

I went to the garage to get some fertilizer, and as soon as I pulled it off the shelf, I heard Laney scream. I came running out of the garage and found Laney and Hekate standing about three feet back from one of the raised beds. Both Meri and Bonkers were perched on the edge of the bed staring at something.

From my vantage point, I couldn't see what they were looking at until I got much closer. When I finally saw what they were all upset about, it nearly took my breath away.

"You guys get back," I barked. "Meri, Bonkers, get down from there."

It was silly because the death beetle wriggling around in the dirt couldn't hurt Meri... but I wasn't so sure about Bonkers. Meri batted at the beetle, and it let out a little hiss. That was enough to send Bonkers scrambling to Laney's feet, but it only made Meri... and Hekate, get closer.

I stepped between my daughter and the death beetle. "Meri, stop," I said as I examined the silver skull that looked painted on its back. But the image wasn't painted on. The beetles were magically bred to have it, and to be both harbinger and carriers of death. And sometimes destruction.

Why was one in my garden?

"Hi. My name's Bert," a voice said, and it took me a moment to realize that the death beetle had just introduced herself.

A female death beetle? I racked my brain for any crumb of knowledge about magical creatures. It was an aspect of the magical arts I hadn't studied too much… Especially when it came to bugs. Ugh, I shuddered at the memories of my brief study of mystical creepy-crawlies.

But I was able to remember that's why the skull on her… on Bert's back was silver. Male death beetles had a red skull. It was then that I also remembered that the males were used as harbingers of death because they were otherwise basically useless. The females were the most potent magically and were actually used to kill.

The females. Like the one still wriggling around in the garden bed.

What was I going to do? I couldn't just touch it. I was a witch, sure, but that thing... Bert... was still dangerous.

"Meri," I started to say, but then Bert piped up again.

"Please don't," she said realizing the danger she suddenly found herself in because of my evil-, ghost-, and demon-destroying familiar.

I should have just ignored her, but something about the distress in Bert's squeaky little voice tugged at my heart. I stayed between the death beetle and my daughters, but I was prepared to hear Bert out.

For some reason...

"You're going to have to tell me fast why we shouldn't eliminate you immediately," I said. "Because right now you are putting my daughters in danger and my patience is thin."

"I'm no danger to you," Bert said. "I was bound to another witch, and now that I've served my purpose, I just wanted a quiet retirement. Your garden seemed like a nice place. I'm sorry. I guess I thought it would be okay."

"Mom," Laney said and tugged on my arm. "We can't kill her. She just wants to be our friend."

"What is wrong with you?" Hekate directed at her sister. "That's a death beetle."

"I would think that would be right up your alley," Laney shot back.

Hekate thought it over for a moment. "You're actually right. Mom, can we keep her?"

What was happening?

"We need to back this up a little bit," I said. "I want to hear more about you being bound to another witch and serving your purpose. Because my Auntie was murdered recently, and I'm wondering if you had something to do with that?"

"Oh, yeah, Lilith. See, everything is fine. She's gone, and I'm retired," Bert said.

"Okay, first of all, it's not fine because she's my Auntie. Second of all, how are you still here? You should have taken her over to the other side."

"Right, but see, she died and then she was gone. I didn't have to take her over to the other side, so I got to stay."

"But how?" I demanded.

"I don't know. I'm a beetle," Bert said as if it were the most obvious thing in the world.

"Well, who spelled you?" I asked as calmly as possible. After all, none of this was actually Bert's fault.

"What's going on, guys?" Thorn's voice startled all of us.

"Eeeeek!" Bert shrieked and then burrowed down into the garden dirt.

"There's a death beetle, Daddy!" Hekate yelled and then ran over to him.

Not to be left out, Laney went sprinting after her.

He looked at me as they crashed into his arms. "A death beetle?"

"It's exactly what it sounds like," I said, and then crossed the yard to join them. "But don't worry, it's spelled to kill one person, and that wasn't any of us."

"Sounds intense," Thorn said. "Are you sure we're okay? I was planning on cooking out tonight."

"We just cooked out, Daddy," Laney said.

"Yeah, but the weather is perfect," he said and ruffled her hair. "And I just like doing it."

"Yes, please. Let Daddy cook dinner if he wants," I said and kissed him.

"Can you wrap some corn on the cob and a few baked potatoes?" he asked. "And then I can do all of the cooking."

"I can do that!" Hekate volunteered and then ran through the back door.

"I'll help so she doesn't get butter everywhere," Laney offered.

"Can you put some of that cotija cheese and chili pepper on two of them?" I asked her.

"And lime?" Laney asked.

"That would be perfect," I said.

"And I'll grab some chicken and burgers from the fridge," Thorn said. "You don't have to do a thing."

"You guys are the best. We were going to have tater tot casserole, but if you're going to cook, we'll do that tomorrow night instead."

Once they were inside doing their grill prep, I wandered back out to the garden. I wasn't done talking to Bert yet, and I hoped she'd come back out and talk to me again.

I searched for a minute and found her munching on the leaves of Hekate's belladonna plant. "You probably shouldn't eat that," I said without thinking.

"It's fine," she said with a shrug. I mean, if beetles could shrug…

"Makes sense," Meri said as he jumped onto the frame of the raised garden bed.

191

Bonkers had gone inside with Laney, but Meri had stayed outside with me.

"I guess you're right. A death beetle would live on poison, right?"

"Means nothing can eat me," Bert said.

"I could still eat you," Meri groused.

Bert stopped chewing her bite of leaf and gaped at him.

"I won't though," he clarified.

"So, can I stay?" Bert asked. "I like this place. I mean, as long as this cat doesn't eat me."

"I prefer bacon," Meri said.

"He's not going to eat you," I said. "We feed him too well around here for him to eat bugs in the garden."

"But can I stay?" Bert asked.

"On one condition," I found myself saying.

"What's that?"

"You have to tell me who you killed and who sent you to kill them," I said.

"You already know who I killed. I killed Lilith," Bert said. "Well, sort of. You know how it is. The poison killed her, but I did my death beetle thing. Well, other than taking her over to the other side… I showed up, and that's what matters."

"Oh, right. But who sent you to kill her?" I asked and waited with anticipation.

The whole case was about to be blown open by a beetle in my garden. Thorn and the girls would have the cookout, and I would go bring her killer to justice.

Bert didn't say anything. She opened her mouth and closed it about three times. Then, she finally said, "I can't tell you that."

"That's my condition for you living here," I reminded her. "Why can't you tell me? If you do, you can stay here for the rest of your life. When it gets cold in the winter, you can cozy up in the garage or the basement."

"No, I mean I can't tell you," Bert said with defeat. "Not that I don't want to… or that I shouldn't… I mean that I can't. I open my mouth to say her name, and nothing comes out."

I looked at Meri. Meri looked back at me and swished his tail. I felt all the wind go out of my sails.

"It was part of the spell," I said.

"You believe me?" Bert asked hopefully.

"I do," I said.

"Maybe we can break the spell," Meri said.

"Please don't hurt me," Bert squeaked.

"We can do it without hurting you," I assured. "I can, anyway."

"Okay," Bert said cautiously. "But then I can stay?"

"I think it's a fair trade," Meri added. "Since she can't actually tell you who sent her."

"Does this even matter?" I asked. "I mean, Lilith was poisoned. So, Bert here was sent for what? To make sure the poison worked? As a backup?"

"It means you don't need to investigate any regular people anymore," Meri said.

"Maybe?" I pondered that. "But it could have been a coincidence too, right? If anything, I've learned that a lot of people had it out for Lilith."

"Pretty big coincidence," Meri snarked.

"I know, but until we know, we just don't know," I said. "Okay, let's do a little ritual and see if we can figure out who sent her."

While Thorn was grilling, the girls, Bonkers, Meri and I set up a protection circle on the patio.

Bert waited in the center munching on some sweet pepper strips Laney got for her from the fridge. I ringed a seven-foot area in a thin circle of salt. Once we closed ourselves into the circle, the girls set up five sets of three small blue candles.

"That's a lot," Thorn commented as he flipped the chicken.

"This is important," I said as I lit a bunch of sage.

"You're the professional," he said and winked.

"Yeah, Mom's the best witch," Laney said.

"She could be the most powerful in the world if she wasn't so…" Hekate started to say.

Thorn cut her off. "Your mom knows what she's doing. You should respect that."

"Sorry, Mom," Hekate said and ground the toe of her shoe into the patio.

"It's okay," I said. "You'll understand more when you're older. But for now, how about you help your sister light all of the candles. I want to know who killed Lilith before dinner is ready."

Once the candles were lit, and Bert had finished her pepper snack, we started the ritual. It was pretty basic. We lit the candles, placed the herbs, and the closed the circle.

I then called upon Bert to tell me who had sent her to kill Lilith. When she could tell me, I whispered an incantation to break the spell.

And that's when things went south. The sage bundle flared up like someone dumped gasoline on it, and I ended up dropping it outside of the circle. I didn't mean to, but it burned my hand. I healed it quickly, but it still hurt.

Then the candles turned black. Dark clouds blew in, and thunder crashed overhear.

I watched as Thorn quickly gathered the food off the grill onto large platters and carried it inside.

"What's going on?" Bert asked.

"A dead witch's spell," Laney said when it dawned on her what was going on.

With that, lightning flashed and the sky opened up. The pouring rain washed our protection circle away, but it didn't matter. We were done anyway.

The girls ran into the house with the familiars. I dispersed our circle with a quick spell.

As far as Burt, she skittered off and dug into the dirt around the foundation of the house. With her hiding away and safe, I ran inside too.

"It doesn't make any sense," Meri said as we sat down to eat the meal Thorn had cooked out for us.

"Tell me about it."

"What are you going to do?" Meri asked.

"For now, I'm going to eat my dinner. After that, I don't know. I've got to figure out who else died."

Chapter Thirteen

The next morning, I dropped the girls off at school and headed into Craft Donuts to get a dozen donuts. My plan was to bribe mall security into letting me see some of the security footage from the morning Lilith died. That way, I could at least cross Druella off my list of suspects. I also hoped that if there was another dead witch in Coventry, I'd hear the gossip.

I looked over our selection for the day and tried to figure out which donuts a security guard would like the best. I had no idea. Nor did I know if a person's job even influenced what types of donuts they liked. In the end, I went with a wide assortment. I had everything from Boston cream to raspberry jelly with peanut butter icing. Oh, and our shop specialties were ghost-shaped donuts with vanilla icing and witch hat-shaped donuts with purple berry frosting. I made sure to include a couple of those too.

While I was taping up the box, a customer came in and stared at me. My other employees were in the back, and it was just me behind the counter. As soon as I noticed the woman, I put on a smile and said, "Welcome to Craft Donuts, how can we delight you today?" Sure, it was cheesy, but the customers loved it.

The woman opened her mouth to speak but then closed it quickly. She looked like she was about to say something else... and then burst into tears.

At first, I wasn't quite sure what to do. Seconds later, I snapped out of it and put my box of donuts down on the counter. I rushed around to the woman.

"Are you okay? What can I do to help?" I asked as I put a comforting hand on her shoulder.

Chalfy appeared from the back. He grabbed some napkins and handed them to me. I handed them over to the woman.

"I'm sorry," she said and sniffled. "I don't mean to be so dramatic."

"It's okay," I said. "Do you want some coffee and a donut?"

"I guess that's why I came in," she said and blew her nose on a couple of the napkins.

"Chalfy, can you grab her a coffee and one of today's specials?"

"How did you know which donut I wanted?" the woman asked.

"I own a donut shop. I have a sense for these things," I said.

She calmed down a little, wiped her nose again, and then dried the tears under her eyes. By the time the woman had thrown away her napkins, Chalfy had her coffee and donut.

"I really wanted to talk to you," she said as she took her breakfast.

"Okay," I headed behind the counter to grab myself a coffee. "I have a few minutes," I said over my shoulder to her.

Before I joined the woman at her table, I grabbed myself a donut too. I figured if I was going to stick around, I might as well have one.

"So, you know who I am," I said as I sat down across from her. "I'm sorry, but I don't think we've officially met, though."

"Lucinda," she said. "We haven't met, but I know of your family. I mean that you guys are sort of famous around here, so I know who you are. Plus, I love this shop."

"Thank you," I replied. "You said you wanted to talk to me?"

"I'm sorry about your great-aunt's passing," she said.

"That's very kind of you."

"I've been torturing myself since her death wondering if I should tell you what I saw."

"What you saw? You know something about her death?"

"I don't know. That's why I wasn't sure if I should talk to you. I keep going back and forth."

"Tell me," I said and tried not to sound too demanding.

"Okay, this is all going to sound weird, but I saw her the day before she died."

"That doesn't sound weird at all. I'm sure a lot of people saw her." I was completely confused.

"I mean that I think I saw something. See, I hike in the woods around Coventry several times per week. And the day before your great-aunt died, I saw her out in the woods."

"I guess that is a little strange. Hiking wasn't her thing. But maybe she just wanted some fresh air."

"I would think the same thing except that the area where I saw her wasn't easy to get to. It's not a place someone taking a casual stroll would find themselves. And she was acting strange."

"Strange how?" I asked.

"Well, she was spinning."

201

"Spinning?" I asked.

"Yeah, like in circles. With her arms out. Oh, and she was talking to herself."

Neither of those things sounded that strange for Lilith. I could see how someone outside our family might think it was weird, but I knew her too well. Spinning in the woods and talking to herself was probably the most normal thing she did that day.

"Lilith was quirky," I answered. "You shouldn't beat yourself up over hesitating. She might have just been dancing and singing in nature."

"I could see that," Lucinda said. "But there's more. Every once in a while, she stopped talking and spinning. She stooped down and picked something off the ground, and I could have sworn she was eating it."

Again, I could see how all those things together might make someone think Lilith was behaving strangely, but I could still dismiss it all as Lilith being Lilith. "Do any berries grow in that area? Or thistle?" I'd actually seen Lilith plucking the little purple flower petals from thistle flowers and sucking the nectar from them.

"I suppose there are both," Lucinda admitted.

"See," I said and took a sip of my coffee. "I thank you for coming to talk to me, but I'm sure it was just her being weird. But not in a way that would get her killed. Just her usual quirks."

"She must have been in really good shape to get out there," Lucinda insisted. "I sometimes struggle to get to that area."

Lucinda didn't know that Lilith was a witch. She didn't know that even if Lilith wasn't as spry as someone sixty years younger than herself, she could always use magic to assist her.

But before I could give another excuse, Lucinda's phone rang. She took it out of her purse and glanced at her screen. "I'm sorry, but I have to take this. Thanks for talking to me, and if you have any other questions, you can always ask. I'm in here most days, and I work over at the farm store. I'm their bookkeeper, so if you come in, you'll have to ask for me. But they'll get me."

"Thank you so much," I said, and Lucinda excused herself.

I sat at the table and finished my coffee and a donut while I mulled over my trip to the mall. Once I was done, I cleaned off my table, checked with my staff to make sure they didn't need anything, and then set out for the mall in the next town over.

I put the donuts in the back seat because despite the fact that I told him he couldn't go into the mall, Meri had insisted on coming along. I also had another coffee to sip on stuck in the cup holder between the front seats. I didn't need another coffee, but since when did that ever stop anybody?

Chapter Fourteen

As I suspected, the mall was dead. Nobody went to the mall anymore anyway, and during the day during the week, it was a ghost town. I pulled into a parking spot close to the building and set the pet mode on the car for Meri. It kept the car a comfortable temperature while keeping it locked. Not that anybody could steal Meri...

After grabbing the box of donuts, I made my way to the doors. Inside, the air was still, but cool, and music drifted from ancient speakers.

The section I'd entered joined with another larger wing of the mall about a hundred feet in front of me. There I found a giant map of the mall. I had an idea of where the security office was from previous trips to the mall, but I located it on the map just to be sure.

Once I was confident where I was going, I set out and found the security office within a few minutes. A few very depressing minutes.

So many of the stores were empty. They looked like missing teeth with their lights out and vacant fronts. Most of the stores that were open were empty except for one person working behind the counter. And the majority of those shops were names I'd never heard before. Probably local businesses trying to take advantage of the reduced rent, but they would ultimately fail too. At least in the mall location. What good was cheap rent if there were no customers?

I felt bad and tried to throw a little luck their way as I passed. A few even looked up and smiled. Maybe if they couldn't make it there, they'd go on to do even bigger and better business elsewhere.

When I found the security office, I wasn't quite sure what to do. Did I knock? Should I just go in?

It didn't occur to me until I pushed through the glass door that the guard, or guards, might not even be in there. They should've been out patrolling the mall.

Fortunately for me, Dwight was not. He was in the office with his feet up on an old metal desk with a scuffed wood top. Whether that wood was real or not would be up for debate. I heard the sound of Candy Cronchers drifting from the phone he held six inches from his face, and it took him a good minute to realize I'd even entered the office.

"You shouldn't be in here," he said and quickly set the phone face down on the desk.

He reeled back and nearly fell trying to get his feet off the desk. His laid-back posture had disguised most of his ample belly, but it now flopped over the top of his uniform pants, its girth straining the bottom button of his shirt precariously.

"Why not?" I asked casually. "I have a security matter."

"Oh, well, okay," he said like he'd never had to deal with any kind of matter in his tenure as a mall security guard. "We don't get much action around here. How can I help?"

"I'm sure you don't," I said and regretted it when he looked wounded. "What I mean is, it's very quiet here. You must run a tight ship."

"Actually, I guess I do," he said and puffed his chest out while polishing the nails of his right hand against his shirt.

I feared that bottom button was going to give up the ghost, and when it did, someone could lose an eye. A chuckle stuck in my throat as I imagined it sailing through the air… finally free.

"I can see that," I said piling on the flattery after seeing it was my way in. It usually was. That and donuts.

"You said you had a matter you needed assistance with?" As he said this, his eyes drifted down to the box of donuts in my hands.

I had him. Hook. Line. Sinker.

At least, I thought I did.

"I'm looking into a crime back in my town. Coventry. It's a few miles from here."

"I know Coventry," he said. "Never been there, but I've heard you guys do a booming tourism business for such a small town."

"That we do," I confirmed. "But we've had… an issue lately. And someone… a suspect…said that she was here mall walking when the deed was done. I was just hoping I could take a teeny tiny peek at your security footage for that morning and see if she was, in fact, here walking."

"Are you law enforcement?" Dwight said and stiffened.

I felt the line go slack.

"My husband is the sheriff in Coventry," I answered.

"You mean the county sheriff?"

"No, he's the town sheriff. It's a whole thing. The mayor is thinking of converting the department over to the Coventry Police Department, but that's not something you care about right now…" I trailed off.

"But your husband is law enforcement, and you work for him?"

I bleated out a laugh and then stifled it quickly. I was going to lose the guy if I didn't reel him back in fast.

"I brought donuts," I said and thrust the box in his direction. "I own the donut shop there, Craft Donuts. Best in the state, if I do say so myself. And no, I'm not law enforcement, but I'm assisting in the case. Like a consultant."

"What kind of case?" Dwight asked skeptically, but he took the box of donuts.

"Let me level with you," I said and lowered my voice to a conspiratorial whisper. "It's a murder investigation. And you, Dwight, could help me bring a killer to justice."

His eyes went wide. "Really?"

I had him again.

"Yes! The information on your security cameras is vital to my investigation. It could be the thing that breaks the case."

He opened the box of donuts and looked them over for a second before turning back to me. "Look, ma'am, thank you for the donuts, but I can't help you. I can't just let some lady off the street look at security footage. You need, like, a warrant or something. Don't you?"

"Not if you let me look at them," I said, but I actually had no idea. "I just need to see a few minutes of footage from a couple of days ago. Either my suspect," and I tried to say that part all official like, "is there or she's not. And if she's not, we can make an arrest," I lied.

Because Lilith's death hadn't even been ruled a murder officially. When I found the murderer, there'd be no arrest. I'd handle it myself. But Dwight didn't need to know that.

He thought it over, and then reached for a donut. And I knew I was going to get to look at that footage. Even if he hadn't said as much yet, him taking a donut was the same as him accepting my terms.

"I don't know," he said as he looked one of the ghost donuts over.

"Please, Dwight. It's dedicated professionals like you that help crack these cases wide open. You could be a hero, and I'm sure it's perfectly legal for you to let me look at that footage." I was laying it on a little thick, but I needed him to say yes before he thought about it too hard.

Just then, his walkie cracked. I jumped a little, and Dwight looked equally as shocked. "I'm sorry, hold on a second," he said and set the donut back in the box. "Nobody ever calls me on this thing."

He stepped a few feet off to the side and had a conversation with someone about a disturbance at the Victoria's Secret. Because of course that store was still in the mall. Victoria's Secret could never die, and of course, there was a disturbance there. I could only imagine…

"I've got to go check this out," he said. "What an exciting day. Nothing ever happens at this job."

"I bet," I replied.

"Look, I don't know about all of this, but I don't want to be responsible for a killer walking free. The security command center is back through that door," he said and thumbed over his shoulder. "I'm not saying that you can go back there and look over the footage you're looking for, but it's not locked or anything. Just be gone when I get back… and leave the donuts."

I waited until he'd left the office and headed through the door to the "command center." The name was hilarious given what I found. It was a long folding card table with a ten-year-old computer and four crappy monitors. Someone had taken the time to set two of the monitors up on old textbooks so they sat above the other two.

It wasn't exactly a high-end setup, and the keyboard gave me the heebie-jeebies. Since no one was around, I used a bit of magic to clean and sanitize the keyboard and mouse before I touched them.

Finding the footage wasn't that hard. The only things on the computer were files from the cameras and a web browser. For a moment, I wondered what I'd find in that browser history, but I knew I didn't want to know.

I clicked on the files and found the date Lilith died. It was a good thing I'd come when I did because it looked like the system didn't keep old footage much past seventy-two hours.

After about five minutes of watching one of the cameras from the day Lilith died, I spotted Druella and her "friends" walking laps around the mall. If you didn't know that there were problems in their little group, you'd have never guessed it by looking at them. They were all laughing and talking, and I felt a stab of sadness for her. It would be terrible to be shut out of your support system like that. Even Pinky looked happy. Part of me knew that was a mask, though. It disguised a horrible human being.

I had to wonder why the owner of Sew Crafty even employed that vile woman. Maybe I'd have to sit down with her for a chat...

But that was for another time. I'd seen what I'd come to see, and it was time for me to take my leave of the mall security office before Dwight came back. I'd had about enough of him for the day too, and who knew how he'd react if he came back to find me still lingering in his "command center."

My stomach growled as I walked through the office to the glass door between me and the main mall. Using magic to clean that keyboard had been enough to make me hungry again, and I wished I'd kept one of those donuts. Or that Dwight had left them behind.

Why had he taken them with him to check on a disturbance? I shook my head. Not my circus, and certainly not my monkey. I pushed my way through the door into the mall and nearly shrieked.

"You look like you've seen a ghost," Lilith said with a chuckle. "I don't think I'm ever going to get tired of that joke. So sorry, dear. Did I scare you?"

"You just startled me," I said and pressed my hand to my chest as if it could slow my galloping heart. "I wasn't expecting anyone to be right outside the door. I almost ran into you… or hit you with the door. Or both."

"I had plenty of room," she said with a shrug and then did not elaborate.

"Lilith, what are you doing here?" I asked when she didn't say anything else. "Did you follow me to the mall?"

"Maybe I'm just here to do a little shopping," she protested.

"Have you ever even been to the mall before? Have you ever gone to any mall in your life?" I was skeptical.

"That's not the point."

"That's exactly the point, Lilith. I mean, it's fine if you did follow me here… I guess. A little weird. Why didn't you just ask to come along?"

"I didn't follow you here," she maintained.

Realizing that arguing with her about it, even though I knew she'd followed me to the mall, was going to get me nowhere, I dropped it. "Okay. Sure, then. So, what's up then? Were you waiting for me outside the security office?"

"Yes," she admitted and twirled one of her blood-red curls around her finger. "I mean, I happened to be here shopping, and I saw you go in there. So, I decided to wait for you."

"Okay," I said.

"And you said you were going to come over to my house to get burgers yesterday, and you never showed up."

"Oh, man. I'm so sorry," I said and genuinely felt bad. "I just got so busy, but that's no excuse. I really am sorry, Lilith."

"That's okay," she brightened. "Why don't you buy me a pretzel and we'll call it even."

"That does sound good. The food court is this way," I said and started walking off to our right.

"Lead the way."

Once we got our pretzels and a couple of sodas, Lilith and I sat down at one of the many empty tables. I'd ordered a jumbo soft pretzel with cheese dipping sauce, and Lilith had gotten a pizza pretzel and an order of pretzel dogs. I stole one, and while she looked as if she'd protest, she ultimately let it slide.

"Don't worry, if you want more, I'll buy you another order," I said when her bottom lip jutted out a little.

That same feeling returned from the other night. I hated that all she had to do was pout a little and I was ready to jump to her bidding, but I also got completely taken in by her.

"You'll have to teach me that spell," I said before tearing off a piece of my pretzel and dipping it in the cheese sauce.

"What spell?" she asked innocently, and I could swear her eyes sparkled.

"The one you're using to bewitch everyone around you," I said flatly. "You know, you're beautiful enough without using enchantments."

"I have no idea what you're talking about."

"I'm not blind," I said softly. "I can see how everyone jumps to do whatever you want. Even Dorian. And he's gay, Lilith. I'm pretty sure he was half in love with you the other night. Also, there's a little matter of how jealous I suddenly feel around you. Like I'm not good enough. It's not something I ever felt with the old Lilith."

"That Dorian character is half in love with you too," she protested.

"That's different," I maintained.

"Is it now?"

"We love each other, but it's not like that. Not at all. And you're doing it again. You're twisting me up. I don't get it. Why?"

"I'm sorry, Kinsley, dear. I'm just having a little fun. I guess it's not right, and I'll stop. Well, I'll stop around you. No promises with anyone else, and yes, I can teach it to you."

"Thank you," I said and felt myself relax. "So, what did you want to talk about?"

"What makes you think I have an agenda?"

"Lilith, level with me. You said you didn't follow me to the mall, and that's fine. But you were waiting for me outside of the security office. I don't think you have an agenda," that was a lie because I knew she did, "but I do think you've got something on your mind."

Lilith shoved a pretzel dog nugget in her mouth, and I waited patiently for her to chew and swallow it. I had to wonder what could be causing the "queen of demons" to clam up like she was, but I casually tore off another piece of my pretzel and dunked it in the cheese sauce.

When she was finally done chewing, she said, "I think you should stop investigating my death."

"What?"

"I mean, that's what you were here doing, right?" she asked.

"Well, yeah. I was checking on Druella's alibi. It's airtight, by the way. She was here walking when you... died. So, now I need to focus on other suspects."

"But that's the thing, Kinsley. You don't need to focus on anything but your life. You've got a Coven to run, those precious girls to raise, and the hunkiest

217

of husbands to keep you busy. You don't need to be out here bribing rent-a-cops at the mall."

"I didn't bribe him," I protested even though I totally had.

"I saw him leave the office with a box of Craft Donuts, Kinsley."

"Fine, I bribed him with some donuts. I'd do anything for you or any other member of my family, Lilith. I have to find out who killed old you."

"But again, you don't. I'm fine. I'm better than fine, Kinsley. I'm renewed, and I feel so good. The person who offed old me did me a favor," Lilith said before taking a slurp of her soda.

"You might look at it that way, but I don't. There's a witch killer on the loose, and it's my job to stop them."

"I believe you are seriously overthinking this, Kinsley. No one is in any danger. I was the target, and what's done is done. We're all-powerful witches, and even though I don't think the killer is going to go after anyone else, we can stop them if they do," she answered with a sigh.

"I can't accept that. They got to you, and that means they might be able to get to any of us."

"That's just not true," Lilith said.

"How?"

"Because I was old and weak. I was past my time. I know you and the rest of my sisters will never admit it, but it's the truth. Plus, we know now. There's no element of surprise. We're all watching each other's backs. It's time to let this go."

"It's not," I said and stood up. "Do you need a ride?"

"I have a ride. It's how I got here," she said. "But Kinsley, don't go."

"You can have the rest of my pretzel," I said and slid it across the table to her.

"Are you angry with me, dear?" Lilith asked.

"No, I'm not. I just need to go. I've got a lot of work to do and limited time to do it. You don't want me taking time away from my girls or Thorn, then I've got to do my investigating during the day while they are gone."

"What about spending time with me?" she asked, and there was the faintest glimmer of hurt in her eyes.

"Come over tonight for dinner, Lilith. Come spend time with all of us. The girls would be thrilled."

"I will do that, then," she said.

"I'll see you tonight."

And with that, I left her to finish the pretzel feast. I'd need to stop somewhere else and get more to eat because I wasn't full. But I had to get out of there. I wasn't angry with Lilith at all, but I was upset. I was frustrated. And I didn't want to end up taking it out on her. She might want me to let her murder go and move on with life, but I just couldn't do that.

I was almost out the doors and back outside when something dark darted in my direction from the children's play area. The fluffy shadow skittered across the polished floor and nearly collided with me.

"I meant to do that," Meri said and resumed sauntering next to me.

"Sure, you did," I said. "I thought you were going to wait in the car. I don't think the mall allows cats."

"Don't see anybody around to even care," he said and was completely right.

"You wanted to stay in the car."

"You locked me in," he said as we crossed the parking lot to the car. "So, I had to break out. Plus, you were taking too long. And I smell pretzels on you. You reek of butter and salt... and cheese sauce. Where's mine?"

"I didn't think you'd want any," I said with a shrug. "And I locked you in the car for your own safety. Didn't want anybody trying to steal you."

"You owe me a delicious meal."

I was going to protest but instead agreed. "I'm hungry too."

"Didn't get enough pretzel? I didn't get any at all."

"You're so dramatic. And no, I didn't get enough. I got upset and gave the rest to Lilith."

"Lilith is here? Why did you give her your pretzel instead of me?"

"Get in the car."

I explained everything to him as we drove to the nearest burger joint.

Chapter Fifteen

After a burger and fries for me and three orders of bacon for Meri, eaten in the car because I couldn't take him into the restaurant, we left for the orthopedic clinic.

In the future, I decided to drive the extra few minutes to a restaurant owned by witches so Meri could go in with me. Most likely no one would have noticed if I had taken him in, but I didn't want to chance it. Plus, our time in the car gave me a chance to figure out where I wanted to go next. Meri was a good sounding board when he was noshing on bacon and couldn't tell me how stupid I was being.

He just told me that on the way to the clinic. "You should maybe consider listening to Lilith," he protested as I pulled into the parking lot.

"What? Why? There's a killer on the loose, Meri. Have you all gone insane?"

"I know you're going to say that this is your business because you're the head of the coven, but maybe consider that it's not really your business. It was Lilith that died, and she wants you to leave it alone."

"I can't believe you," I said in shock. "Where is this coming from?"

"I'm bored," he said and yawned. "There has to be something more interesting to do with our afternoon than visiting an orthopedic clinic, Kinsley."

I rolled my eyes. "You're unbelievable. You're trying to talk me out of solving a murder because you're bored... For a second, I thought you really were going soft."

"Hey, watch it, lady. My fur is very soft indeed, but that's it."

"You're going to have to wait outside."

"Boo!"

"Meri, it's a doctor's office."

"Bored."

"Then go do something else. I can handle this."

"Fine. Maybe I will."

"Fine."

I rolled my eyes again and headed into the clinic. When I looked back over my shoulder, Meri was still sitting outside on the sidewalk staring daggers at me.

I'll spare you the boring details of my conversation with Aileen. Apparently she never saw anything at Wayde Barlow's farm. She has some serious mental health issues, and for a while, she was off her meds.

223

"There's a garden out there for sure, but it's nothing strange. Not too strange anyway," she said while looking around to make sure none of the patients or her coworkers were listening in to our conversation.

"Well, thank you for talking with me. I'm sorry I bothered you at work."

"And I'm sorry for your loss. I feel terrible that I spoke badly of her in my… state."

"It's all right," I replied. "We all go through things."

When I got back outside, Meri was still sitting on the sidewalk waiting for me. He started following me back to the car without a word.

"I thought you were leaving," I finally said as I opened the car door for him to get in.

"Whatever. I want to be around when you do stupid stuff. Could be any minute now."

"You're the worst."

"I can't be because you are," Meri said as he settled into the passenger seat.

"Whatever."

"Whatever… What are we doing now?" Meri asked with a sassy flick of his tail.

"I'm not sure what to do next," I said and bit my bottom lip. "I mean, maybe we could go see if Wayde Barlow is around? I'm not sure if I have any other leads to go on."

"We could go home and eat bacon," Meri suggested.

"Wayde Barlow's farm it is."

"Bummer."

"And then bacon. Besides, maybe that will be the lead that solves the case and then we'll need to celebrate."

"Maybe."

"No maybe. That's what we're doing, and I want positive vibes."

"Now you sound like that idiot at the craft store."

"Touché."

We drove out to Wayde Barlow's farm, and I was excited to see a brow Chevy pickup truck parked in front. It hadn't been there before when Thorn and I dropped by, so I thought maybe there was a chance Wayde was home. I was getting out of the car to approach the house when Meri reminded me of something I'd completely forgotten.

"Didn't you hide the last time you were here because you were afraid Wayde wouldn't talk if you're around?"

I froze. I was already out of the car standing there with the driver's side door open. "You know, you could have said something about that before we drove all the way out here."

"What fun would that be?"

"I'm going to go talk to him," I decided. "I'll look completely insane if I just get back in the car and drive off."

"Too late. You already look insane."

"Are you coming or not?" I asked and pretended like I was going to shut the door.

Meri skittered out of the car. "I'm surprised you're letting me out of the car."

"You're so dramatic," I said as we made our way up the driveway and past the brown truck.

We walked up the steps to the covered front porch, and I knocked on the front door. Less than a minute later, a man answered.

"Hello," he said and smiled. "Can I help you?"

"Are you Wayde Barlow?" I asked, but I'd seen him before. I was pretty sure it was Wayde that stood before me, but I wanted to be sure before I launched into my inquiry. Wouldn't want to accuse the wrong farmer of murder or anything like that...

"I am," he said and extended a hand for me to shake. "And you're Kinsley Wilson, right?"

I shook his hand and said, "You know me?"

"Of course, you're practically famous around town."

"I am?"

"Yeah, and well, I'm also a fan of your Aunt Lilith. I'm so sorry for your loss."

"You were a fan of my aunt?" I felt flabbergasted. The conversation was not going at all as I'd have expected.

"You seem surprised," he said.

"I am. I mean, I came out here to talk to you because I heard rumors that you hated Lilith. Mostly because she was blackmailing you into letting her grow poison plants on your farm."

That made him chuckle. "Small-town rumors can be a trip," he said and shook his head. "No, I didn't hate Lilith and she wasn't blackmailing me. Wow, that's a doozy."

"I don't understand. So, there wasn't any bad blood between you two, but you did know her. Do you mind if I ask about the nature of your... friendship?"

"I have had some trouble with poison plants on my farm, but not because Lilith was growing them.

Actually, she'd come out here and help me remove them safely. And one time, one of my cows got into something bad. The vet couldn't save the cow, and Lilith made some sort of concoction that saved Bessie. Your aunt was a treasure."

I left Wayde Barlow's farm in complete shock. I was so perplexed that I pulled off the road and parked in the lot at Mr. John's Diner. I had no intention of going in to get food, but it gave me a place to stop and think. And from the abandoned appearance of the parking lot, I wasn't taking a space from a paying customer.

"We're not eating here, right?" Meri seemed concerned. "I know we don't have anything to celebrate, but we don't have to punish ourselves like this."

"We're not eating here," I confirmed. "I just need to think. I've got nothing else to go on. I just cannot…"

"Maybe it is time to let this go."

"Stop telling me to let this go, Meri. Since when are you a quitter? Oh, wait, it's because you're bored."

Meri sighed. "Fine. I get it. And you're not out of leads."

"What are you thinking?"

"Wasn't there that woman who saw Lilith out in the woods being weird?"

"Yeah, I remember that. But do you really think that's something?"

"What else do you have?"

"Good point. I think I knew the area she was talking about. Should we go out there and look for clues?"

"There might be something out there. Maybe someone was stalking Lilith and they dropped something. I don't know. I want bacon."

"I really don't know what we could possibly find out there that would solve her murder, but you're right. We don't have anything else. If nothing else, a walk in the woods might clear my head."

"That's the spirit," Meri groused. "But what about that bacon?"

"Hiking first and bacon later."

"You're trying to starve me to death," Meri complained.

"We could stop into Mr. John's and get you some bacon," I offered.

"Hiking first. I'd rather die of starvation than food poisoning."

"You're such a drama queen."

There were a few different trailheads near Coventry, and each one of them had a small parking lot. I pulled into the one closest to the place where I thought Lucinda had seen Lilith.

Meri followed me up the trail, and a few times I picked him up to cross a stream. "I should have thought about going home and getting hiking boots," I said as I accidently stuck my foot in some shallow water at the edge of a stream.

"You're such a baby," Meri said, but he flicked his tail and my foot was suddenly dry.

"Thanks," I grumbled and put him back down in the grass. "I think we're almost there."

There was no official trail where we were going, but there was a path worn into the grass by other hikers. I followed it around a grove of trees to the clearing I thought Lucinda had described during our conversation at Craft Donuts.

And I found Lilith sitting in the middle of a patch of mushrooms. For a moment, I thought it was old Lilith, but it was just a trick of the light washing out all of her color.

It was new Lilith, and she was deep in thought studying a mushroom she rolled between her thumb and forefinger. "I'm sorry," she said as we approached.

Not entirely sure what to do, I plopped down onto a patch of grass next to her. "Why are you sorry?" My stomach clenched again because something was wrong with the energy around her.

"I guess I have a bit of a confession," she said and handed me the mushroom she'd been studying.

"What could you possibly have to confess to?" I asked but then realized what type of mushroom she'd handed me.

I dropped it immediately and used a touch of magic to cleanse my hand. Meri sniffed it and hissed. He moved a few feet away from us and stretched out in the sun.

"I just want you to remember that I genuinely tried to get you to stop investigating my death," she said and smiled at me softly.

"You did, but I can't just let a murder go. I thought I'd explained myself well enough. I have to figure out who killed you so that I can bring them to justice."

Lilith studied me for a moment and then stuck out her wrists. "Take me away, Kinsley."

"What are you talking about?" I asked as the cogs in my mind refused to clunk into place.

"At first, I genuinely didn't remember what happened, so please don't think I've been lying to you this whole time," Lilith said.

"Lying to me? About what? If there's information I need to find your killer, I need to know. I don't want anyone else to get murdered."

"No one else is going to get murdered, Kinsley."

"How can you possibly know that?"

"Because I wasn't murdered, dear."

"You're going to have to explain to me like I'm a five-year-old what the heck you're talking about, because I am really confused."

Lilith sighed so hard that I could feel it in my chest. "I killed myself."

"What? Why?"

"I really did mean to talk to you beforehand. I wasn't trying to commit suicide or anything like that. Like, I didn't want to die."

"Then why did you kill yourself? None of this makes any sense."

"My old life had run its course, and in order to be reborn, it had to die."

"Oh… Oh."

"Yeah, but I didn't mean to do it that way and have you find me that way. It was going to be a whole ritual where everyone knew what was going down before I did it. But I made the poison for the ritual ahead of time, and I accidently grabbed it when I was trying to get a drink."

"Lilith, why would you put a ritual poison in a bottle of Diet Coke?"

"I like Diet Coke," she said with a shrug. "I really didn't think I'd get them mixed up. I should have marked the bottle, but I thought I'd remember which one was which."

And with that, I got up and started to walk away.

"Where are you going?" Lilith called after me.

"I just need some time. I need some time to think."

Epilogue

So, Lilith didn't come over for dinner with the girls that night. I guess I didn't expect her, but I was disappointed that she didn't show.

She did show up the next morning, though. My doorbell rang right after Mom took the girls to school, and I found Lilith on my front porch holding two piping hot lattes from the Brew Station.

"Hazelnut, right?" she said and thrust a cup toward me.

"It is my favorite, thank you," I said and took it.

"You're welcome. Are you still mad at me?"

"I was never mad at you," I said and took a sip of the latte. "I was just… overwhelmed."

"Well, the coffee wasn't my only peace offering," she said and smiled like a kid on Christmas morning. Lilith rocked back and forth on her heels like she couldn't contain her excitement.

"Okay, but you don't have to bring me peace offerings. It's really okay. You could have come to dinner last night too. I should have called…"

"Well, this peace offering isn't something I brought."

"Do you want to come in?"

"I would, and I promise I'll come for dinner tonight. I miss the girls."

"You would come in? But?"

"I'm going to take Druella out for breakfast. She doesn't think I stole her dog, and I'm going to let her keep thinking it wasn't me, but I'm going to make amends anyway. She seems lonely and needs a friend."

"That's sweet of you, I guess," I said. "Is that the peace offering?"

"No," she said and clapped her hands. "This is great! Okay, so I came here to tell you that I got rid of those pesky goats."

"What?"

"The goats are gone. You don't have to worry about them anymore."

"Did you kill them?" I gasped and nearly dropped my latte.

"No, silly," she said and laughed heartily.

"Okay, what do you mean you got rid of them? Where are the goats, Lilith? Those were people."

"Yeah, but they sucked. So, I had them rounded up by the good folks at Gretta's Goat Rescue in Belleview. I did have to use a little bit of magic to subdue them, but the volunteers got them all. And now they get to live out their lives in peace at a fabulous goat sanctuary. Anyway, I have to go. I'll see you tonight," Lilith said before bounding down my front steps and heading to her car.

She was already out of the driveway and driving away before what she'd said had fully sunk in.

And that's how I ended up driving to a goat sanctuary to retrieve a herd of magic goats…

Thank you for reading!

Made in United States
North Haven, CT
15 September 2022

24160211R00134